RED EYES

A
NICOLE BERETTI
THRILLER

LUKA T. JACOBS

Some monsters are born in darkness.

Others are made by it.

FROM THE AUTHOR

Dear Reader,

This book means a lot to me.

Red Eyes is more than a cryptid thriller. It's about the weight we carry, the fears that follow us, and the courage it takes to finally face what haunts us. Writing this story took me deeper into Nicole Beretti's past than ever before, exploring the emotional scars that shaped her, and what drove the creature known as *Red Eyes* to become what he is.

If you've been following the series, thank you. If this is your first time picking up one of my books, welcome. I do recommend starting at the beginning of the *Nicole Beretti Thriller Series*, as it will give you the full depth of her story and make this book resonate even more.

I hope this story keeps you turning the pages, gives you something to feel, and maybe even makes you look twice at the tree line.

Happy reading,

Luka T. Jacobs

CONTENTS

PROLOGUE

-1987-

The hare shot left through a spray of ferns, then doubled back so fast Tharak nearly tumbled trying to follow. He growled, adjusted course, and barreled through a patch of deadfall. Veyla was already ahead, her feet silent on the moss, hair streaked with dirt and wind. She didn't even look back. She didn't have to.

They ran low to the ground, barely upright, arms brushing trunks as they cut between trees. The hare darted through a narrow gap beneath a rotting log. Veyla dropped flat and slid under it, kicking up a burst of soil. Tharak leapt over instead, stumbling on the landing. Still, they kept after it.

They followed it across a ridge, through a gulley thick with wet leaves, and up into a stretch of pines where the light slanted sharp through the canopy. The hare zigzagged wildly, but they were gaining.

Veyla veered right to box it in.

Tharak surged forward, cutting left to intercept.

The hare vanished between a cluster of boulders. Tharak followed without thinking, dodging a hanging branch, feet sliding on loose rock as he closed the gap.

The forest stilled.

His foot struck bare dirt where there should have been leaves. He slowed just enough to feel the silence. A snarl rose from the right, low and rough.

They had woken the wrong predator.

The mountain lion burst from the slope. It struck him in the ribs and drove him down. They rolled through leaf litter and roots, limbs locked, claws and fists striking. He shielded his throat as teeth snapped close. Its body was taut with hunger and the raw irritation of being woken. He managed to twist beneath it and drove a fist into its flank. It hissed, slashed at him with a paw, and raked his shoulder.

Tharak shoved upward and kicked, trying to create space. The cat came at him again.

Veyla's roar tore through the trees.

She charged from the brush, grabbed the mountain lion by its tail, and dragged it backward with both hands. The cat let out a high, rasping snarl that cracked into a yowl of panic. Her body turned with the motion, and she flung it into a tree. The impact shook bark loose. The cat landed awkwardly, scrambled to its feet, and vanished into the undergrowth with a final screech.

Tharak sat up, breathing hard, skin streaked with dirt. A thin line of blood ran along his collarbone.

Veyla stepped beside him and stared for a moment. Then she made an abrupt clicking noise in her throat, followed by a low chattering grunt. It was her way of laughing at him.

He scowled and wiped his arm. She mimicked his fall with a sloppy stagger and flicked a clump of dirt at his chest. He bared his teeth in return and shoved her shoulder. She shoved back.

They followed the trail home without speaking. When the path grew familiar again, they ran. Not to escape anything. Just to see who could get there first.

****

The cave sat low along the western slope, hidden beneath a curtain of moss and a tangle of old roots. It opened just above a narrow ledge where the rocks dropped toward the edge of Upper Klamath Lake, Oregon. From there, the water stretched wide and cold, bordered by black pine and broken sky. The cave was not large, but it was deep, and the wind could not reach the back wall. It had been their home for many seasons, and even when they followed the prey south or inland, they always returned.

Tharak and Veyla reached the cave as the last light faded behind the trees. Their father had not yet left. He sat near the mouth of the cave in silence, preparing for the hunt. Tharak stood near the opening, one hand braced against the stone. His knuckles were thick, fingers strong but unscarred. At five years old, he was four and a half feet tall and still growing into his limbs. His bones ached sometimes when the night turned damp. His chest was broad, his hair a dark, coarse brown, longer around the shoulders where it had not yet been smoothed by age. He was the only male child of the family, and he carried a name not given lightly.

Tharak meant the one with blood eyes. It had not been spoken as a curse, nor as a blessing. The elder had seen the color in his eyes when he was born and held him close, sharing an image with the others: light striking water, a wound beneath its surface. Blood in vision. That was how they got their names. Not as sound, but as sense. His mother had accepted it without fear. His father had made no sign of approval or rejection. The name stayed.

The family numbered five. His father, Ruunek, stood taller than the others, broad across the back, and rarely vocal. His gestures were short, steady, and final. His mother, Serah, was quieter still but never uncertain. Her movements were more graceful, and she spoke often with her eyes. His older sister, Veyla, had sharp senses and a fast stride. She was nearing the age to hunt alone. The elder, Mekel, moved slowly but carried weight in thought. Her eyes were cloudy, but she saw more than the others understood.

They didn't always need to communicate with grunts or chatter. Often, understanding passed between them in glances and instinct. When something needed to be shared, that couldn't be shown in movement or sound, they projected images to one another: flashes of memory, felt impressions, or a shared sense of hunger or danger. Tharak was learning to shape his thoughts with clarity, though his images were often jumbled and hard to follow. Mekel once tilted her head at one of his visions and looked away, confused.

That night, Ruunek left to hunt beneath a sky littered with stars, and Tharak went with him.

They said nothing as they moved through the trees, feet silent over pine needles and stone. Ruunek never explained things aloud. He taught by doing. By expecting. He would stop suddenly, his arm firm across Tharak's chest, and point, not with a finger, but with a shift of his jaw or a glance of his eyes. He showed Tharak where to crouch, how to use the dark, how to blend into wind and tree. When Tharak's weight shifted too quickly and a branch cracked beneath his foot, Ruunek did not scold. He looked at him. And Tharak understood. The next time, he stepped lighter.

They tracked a lone swine for most of the night. Ruunek let it lead them deep into the slope before motioning for Tharak to hold. He moved forward on his own, silent as stone, and when the moment came, dropped the creature with a blow that made no sound. When Tharak approached, he then placed his hand briefly on his son's shoulder. It was not praise. It was an acknowledgment. A quiet signal that Tharak was learning, and that was enough.

Ruunek was not cruel, but he was distant. His approval was never spoken. It had to be felt. A tilt of the head. The tightening of his mouth. Tharak craved that recognition even when he didn't want to. He mimicked his father's walk without realizing.

Sometimes, when Ruunek sat alone at the cave mouth before dawn, Tharak would watch him from behind, unsure if the thoughts in his father's head were about the hunt, or about something far older, passed down from those who came before.

****

The next morning, mist clung low across the water. Birds had already passed overhead, and frogs clicked from the reeds. Serah was seated near the rear of the cave, combing her fingers gently through Mekel's hair, untangling it with care as she worked in silence. Veyla crouched near the wall, sorting loose pinecones and broken bones from the night before. Ruunek had returned just before dawn, his presence marked by the heavy swine now resting near the cave's edge.

Tharak was restless, as he often was in the mornings. The hunt was over; the meat had been shared, and now the day stretched ahead without direction. He moved along the cave's edge, barefoot and alert, unable to sit still. Mekel sat beneath Serah's hands, her knees drawn up, long arms resting across them. Though she was being groomed, her attention remained fixed on Tharak as he passed. Around them, claw marks and faded smears clung to the stone walls, left by hands long gone, each mark a story passed down through generations as memory and lesson.

The family's rules were few but fixed. Do not draw attention. Do not leave tracks that speak. Do not forget your trail. And return to the cave before the final light fades, so he could hunt with his father and sister if the signs were right.

Tharak left the cave and climbed down the path they had worn over many seasons, stepping over familiar roots and between the blackened trunks of trees that had once caught fire but lived. The morning air was cool, and the wind carried the scent of wet bark and distant water. A squirrel darted across his path, freezing briefly before vanishing into the underbrush. He did not chase it.

Below, at the edge of the lake, the stones were slick. He crouched to inspect one of the driftwood piles left by a recent storm. Nothing moved beneath it. A few crows scattered as he approached, flapping hard into the branches overhead.

When he returned, Veyla was just arriving from the same ridge, a small rabbit limp in her hand. Serah met her with a quiet sound of approval. Tharak paused near the entrance, watching. She was a few years older, nearly of age to hunt alone, but that didn't mean he liked seeing her succeed when he hadn't. He felt a flicker of annoyance, quickly hidden, though it stirred something piercing in his chest. He wanted to bring something back too. He wanted to be more than just a shadow on the trail behind his father.

As the night deepened and the cave filled with breath and warmth, Tharak lay on his side, eyes half-closed but mind still moving. His father had chosen to hunt with Veyla that night, and though no reason had been given, Tharak felt it settle in his chest like a stone. He didn't think of sleep. He thought of hunts that would one day be his to lead. Of standing tall like his father, of Veyla following him instead of racing ahead. Of Mekel nodding in approval. In the dark, he imagined strength in his limbs and command in his voice.

One day, he would not just return to the cave; he would guide them from it.

CHAPTER 1

Senator Walter Granger had made the three-mile hike up the slope with more effort than he cared to admit. His knees had begun to ache halfway through the second ridge, and his daughter's nonstop questions about bears, bees, and whether their cabin had a toilet had tested his patience in ways congressional hearings never had. By the last mile, Brooke had grown tired and insisted she couldn't go any further. When she started stomping her feet and dragging them through the dirt, it nearly set him over the edge.

At sixty-five, Walter had already raised two grown children. Marrying again to a woman thirty years his junior had been a choice made with full awareness that she would want a child of her own. The idea of starting over, of parenting from scratch at his age, had felt daunting. But he loved her. He had chosen her. And when Brooke arrived, wild-haired and loud from the moment she could speak, he had doted on her. The marriage hadn't lasted, but Brooke had given him a new sense of purpose. She was a handful, no doubt, but she kept him on his toes.

Walter ended up bribing her with the promise of marshmallows and a pack of gummy bears hidden in his pack. She agreed on the condition that she could eat both immediately once they reached the top.

Their packs were dusty and sweat stuck to their necks by the time they made it to the clearing. Walter handed over the promised sweets, and Brooke collapsed onto the nearest flat rock like a hiker who had just conquered Everest. She unwrapped the marshmallows with reverence and declared the gummy bears tasted better than any she'd ever had.

The cabin stood where it always had, though fewer people knew about it now. A square structure of weatherworn timber with a rusted metal roof, it had once served as a fire lookout. Now it sat abandoned and off-record, its windows clouded, its solar panels long broken. Walter had pulled a few strings to access it. The Department of Natural Resources kept the access passcode under digital lock, but he still had friends in the state infrastructure office. A few quiet favors could go a long way when one knew how to phrase the ask.

He had chosen the place for a reason. He had been in the press recently, attention that clung like smoke, and he wanted somewhere private to relax with his daughter without cameras or questions. No reporters. No staff. Just quiet.

It had been his idea to take Brooke here. She had just turned eight. Her mother, Walter's ex-wife, was on a wellness retreat in Sedona with her new husband, a man who wore linen and said words like "aligned energy" without flinching. Walter had offered to take Brooke for the week. No television, no calls. Just trees, birds and time with her father.

She'd been skeptical at first.

"I'm not sure if this was a good idea," Brooke had said, squinting at the trailhead.

"What do you mean?" Walter asked, tightening the strap on her pack.

"You always say stuff is relaxing, and then it turns out to be really boring."

He laughed. "Well, it might be a little boring. But the good kind."

"I already miss pizza."

Even when he showed her the topo map and pointed out the blue streak of lake near the cabin, she had wrinkled her nose. It wasn't until they began the climb, and she spotted a deer halfway up the trail that she started to smile.

Now, twenty-four hours in, they had settled into a rhythm. Brooke collected pinecones and sorted them by size. She built tiny stone fences beside the fire ring and sang to herself without knowing he was listening. Walter spent the evening organizing their gear, boiling water, and writing a few notes on a yellow legal pad. He told himself he wasn't thinking about work, though he kept circling back to the budget meeting he was missing and the land use proposal he'd been forced to postpone.

That morning, after a night of light rain, the woods had taken on a slick hush. The trees looked greener, the air rich with the scent of damp moss and leaf rot. Walter sipped his coffee on the cabin's small porch while Brooke leaned over the edge with a stick, pretending to fish in a puddle. She had a scratch on her shin from yesterday's hike but hadn't complained once.

"You know that puddles aren't real fishing holes, right?" Walter asked.

Brooke shrugged. "Depends on what you're fishing for."

"Oh yeah? What are you fishing for?"

"Secrets."

He raised an eyebrow. "Think you'll catch any?"

She gave him a serious look. "Already did. Something whispered to me."

Walter chuckled, brushing rain from the porch rail. "That was probably your stomach."

They had breakfast together, dried fruit, oatmeal, and a few stale marshmallows she had left over.

"You have to admit," she said through a mouthful, "marshmallows make everything better."

"Even oatmeal?"

"Especially oatmeal."

She told him the birds sounded like they were laughing. He asked her what they were laughing at. She said probably him.

By midmorning, Brooke wanted to explore. He agreed, but only within shouting distance. The forest around the cabin grew wild fast. No real trails, no signs, no hikers. That was part of its appeal.

Walter walked with her at first, pointing out lichen on tree bark, teaching her the difference between cedar and pine.

"This one feels like puzzle pieces," she said, running her fingers along the bark.

"That's cedar. Smells better too."

"Smells like your closet."

She picked up a feather and asked what bird it came from.

He paused, unsure. "Owl."

"Really?"

"Probably."

After half an hour, they circled back. Brooke ran ahead, fearless and light, leaving Walter to follow at a slower pace.

The rest of the day unfolded quietly. She made a fort of fallen branches. He read half a novel and considered taking notes on the budget plan again but didn't. They ate jerky and crackers for lunch. Brooke found a salamander and named it Jeff.

"Jeff looks like a lawyer," she said.

Walter blinked. "That's oddly specific."

"Well, he has lawyer eyes."

That night, they sat by the cold fire ring under a sky scattered with stars.

"Dad," Brooke said, curled beside him, "do you ever get scared?"

He looked down at her. "Sometimes. Why?"

"Because it's really dark here. Like really, really dark."

"That's what makes the stars so bright."

Brooke fell asleep in his lap wrapped in a flannel shirt, her breath slow and even. Walter carried her inside, laid her on the bed, and sat for a while listening to the creaks in the roof and the wind threading through the trees.

It was peaceful. More than he had expected.

But the quiet also left room for thoughts he usually kept buried. Like how fast Brooke was growing, and how little he saw her. He told himself this trip would change that. A way to reconnect. To be something more than a scheduled weekend every second month.

He had no sense, not yet, that they weren't alone out here.

Tomorrow, she wanted to see the lake. He had seen it on the map, a winding blue line no more than a mile west. He figured they would pack a snack and make a day of it. He hadn't noticed the tracks near the clearing. Or the faint musky scent that clung to the undergrowth after dark.

Brooke had.

She had mentioned it offhand before bed, nose wrinkled.

"Dad, the woods smell weird."

He had laughed. "That's what real air smells like."

Neither of them had any reason to believe otherwise.

Yet.

CHAPTER 2

The forest whispered beneath their steps, damp leaves pressing into soft earth, the hush of morning fog settling between the trees. Tharak moved ahead of the others, eyes scanning the ground, attention flitting from track to track. Something small had passed recently, sharp claws, a dragging tail. Not important, but still worth watching. He had gone ahead of his father and sister, leading the way as part of his lesson.

Behind him, his father moved without a sound, a mass of dark hair and muscle. Veyla padded close beside him, sniffing the air and casting glances at the trees. Their mother and the elder had remained near the cave, gathering berries from the field below. The lake fed the clan well when the fish were running, and this season had been generous.

Tharak was meant to lead only until they reached the lake edge, then step aside. It was a lesson. His father gave many. Some with gestures, others with silence. This one was about the route, knowing it, reading it, learning which stones shifted, which hollows held scent, and which trees bled when touched.

He was distracted, not careless, but curious. Something

had moved in the underbrush earlier, small and quick, likely a squirrel or something even slighter. It had crossed their path for only a moment before vanishing toward the ridge, and now Tharak veered quietly from the trail, tracking its movement with measured steps.

The surrounding scent began to shift. A breeze moved through the trees, cool with the chill of morning, brushing along the right side of his face. The water was close, but the wind was not blowing from the lake. He could still feel its presence nearby in the way the ground dipped and in the smell of damp stone, but the breeze carried nothing new. No scent of danger. Only forest, pine and clean earth. Nothing suggested the presence of hairless ones.

He had never seen one up close. Only once, from across a distant ridge, he had watched them move below, small, clumsy figures that made noise without meaning. His mother and father had warned him to stay clear of them. They brought fire. Thunder sticks. Death.

He padded around a bend, passed a birch with its skin peeling in long curls, and lifted his gaze.

Movement at the water caught his eye.

A young female hairless one crouched at the lake's edge. She held a long stick in the water, something silver flickering near its end. Her hair was the color of dried grass in late summer, pale and sun-touched, catching the light like thread. A larger male stood nearby with his arms folded, gaze drifting across the trees but unaware.

Tharak froze.

The hairless ones did not often come this deep into the forest. They usually stayed to the lower trails or open camps far from the clan's paths. His breath held tight in his chest, heart thudding beneath his ribs.

He wasn't scared. He was curious. His eyes locked on the small female's face, studying it with quiet fascination. Her tiny features. Her bright hair. The way she moved.

She turned suddenly, her eyes meeting his.

Then she screamed.

The male turned at once, eyes locking onto Tharak.

He spoke quickly, his voice hard though not loud, and reached into his side covering to pull out something dark and metal. It glinted as it caught the light. A thunder stick.

Tharak had never seen one but knew its power. He had seen what they left behind. Shattered bones. Scorched fur. The metallic scent so strong it choked the air.

He stared at the weapon, then at the male hairless one's face. There was fear there, tightly held beneath a layer of tension, but visible in his eyes. His hands were shaking. The small female clung to his leg now, one arm wrapped around him while the other covered her nose. Her shoulders trembled, and tears streamed down her cheeks as she cried softly, unable to look away.

A low growl rumbled behind Tharak, long, deep, and full of warning.

His father stepped forward, towering over Tharak by a full head, teeth bared and hair bristling across his shoulders. He made no move to strike but did not hide either.

Veyla came next, her posture wide and balanced, her face unreadable as always.

The male hairless one stiffened. He did not raise the thunderstick, but his fingers tightened around it. The small female pressed her face into his side, eyes squeezed shut.

He spoke again, this time quieter, and his gaze moved from Tharak to the others. He reached out to the small one and touched her shoulder, guiding her slowly backward.

They began to retreat, step by cautious step. The thunder stick never lifted. The young female looked back once with wide, glistening eyes, then turned and disappeared into the trees with the male.

Tharak let his breath go.

His father turned toward him, gaze heavy with unspoken judgment. There was no gesture, no sound, but the meaning was clear. Tharak had led them too far without knowing what lay ahead. He had not sensed the danger in time.

Veyla brushed past him and bumped his shoulder with

hers. It might have been teasing. It might have been a warning.

He stayed where he was a moment longer, staring at the spot where the hairless ones had been.

The young one's eyes had been blue, blue like the river ice just before the thaw.

They moved on, and Tharak followed, the scent of the lake fading behind them.

CHAPTER 3

Brooke's sobs came in hiccupping bursts as Walter Granger pulled her along the narrow path. His grip on her wrist was firm but not harsh, urgency guiding his every step. The forest, so peaceful the day before, now loomed with menace. Every branch creak and shifting leaf made him flinch. He kept glancing over his shoulder, eyes scanning the undergrowth for movement, for massive shapes that might be following.

The rest of the trail felt longer than it should have, and the cabin had never seemed so far. Trees closed in from every side, the path no longer a trail but a corridor of unease. Walter jumped at the cry of a bird, then again at the snap of a twig. He hated the way his legs shook, hated that his breath came too fast, hated that he was supposed to be the one protecting her and yet felt completely out of his depth.

He had never felt fear like this. Not during hearings, not during negotiations, not even during the few moments in life that had truly tested him. This was a different kind of fear. Primal. Humbling. It made him feel exposed in a way he didn't know was possible.

When the cabin finally came into view, half-hidden in shadow, he didn't slow. He led Brooke up the steps, pushed open the door, and shut it behind them with a solid thud. Locking it, he shoved a chair under the handle for good measure, then turned and saw Brooke standing near the bed, backpack clutched to her chest like a shield.

"Pack your things," he said, his voice still sharp. "Now."

She hesitated, watching him with wide eyes, then nodded and began stuffing her clothes and toys into her bag with trembling hands.

Walter crossed to the table and dug through his gear bag until he found the satellite phone. The keypad glowed dimly. Stepping outside onto the porch, he closed the door behind him. He didn't want her to hear the desperation in his voice.

The line clicked as the call connected.

"It's Granger," he said. "I need immediate evac. Upper Klamath, fire tower cabin. Two on board. ETA?"

He listened, shoulders tense.

"Make it fast. We'll be ready."

He ended the call and stared into the woods for a long moment, phone clenched in his hand. The quiet was back, heavy and full of memory. This time it didn't feel like peace. It felt like waiting.

They shouldn't exist. His brain kept circling back to that. He had seen them with his own eyes, and it shattered everything he thought he understood about the world. He was a man used to having answers, used to being in control. Out there, he had felt small. Vulnerable. That wasn't just frightening. It made him angry.

Back inside the cabin, he kept the gun within reach. Brooke sat on the bed, hugging her bag, her eyes never leaving him. Outside, the forest seemed to hold its breath. He watched the window, every shadow suspect, every breeze a warning.

He paced the floor while Brooke sat crying softly, her small shoulders shaking as she tried to stay quiet. There was nothing he could say to comfort her. He didn't have the words. He wasn't even sure he believed they were safe now.

It was almost an hour before the sound came, distant at first, the chop of rotors sweeping across the treetops. Walter stood and pulled the curtain aside, exhaling sharply when he saw it approaching. The black helicopter circled once before descending into the clearing, sending debris into the air.

He opened the cabin door.

"Let's go."

Brooke was on her feet immediately, her pack slung over one shoulder. He led her outside and across the clearing as a crew member stepped out to help them in.

Once aboard, Walter looked down at the cabin. The trees swallowed it quickly as they rose.

At the landing pad, he guided Brooke into the waiting car and closed the door behind her. Then he stepped a few paces away and raised the phone to his ear.

A voice answered.

Walter's tone was low and charged.

"They were real," he said. "Massive. Covered in hair. Not bears. Not anything I've ever seen. They saw us. They approached us. If I hadn't had my gun, they would've taken her. Or worse, killed us both."

He turned his back to the car, his hand pressed to his forehead.

"I want them hunted. You hear me? Not tagged, not studied. Hunted. Wiped out. They shouldn't exist. I want them gone. Eliminated."

There was a pause as he listened.

"I'm not crazy. I know what I saw. These things are out there. If they're in my state, near my daughter, then they are a threat. Do not fail me."

Another pause.

"Good. Keep me posted."

He ended the call and stood still for a moment, the phone clenched tightly in his hand. Then he turned back to the car and slid into the seat beside Brooke without saying another word.

CHAPTER 4

Night settled deep across the forest. The trees stood still, wrapped in shadow, their breath rising in mist above the needles. Tharak walked between his father and Veyla, each step taken in silence, his eyes adjusting to the pale silver light that spilled through the canopy. The world was different at night. Every sound clearer, every scent layered.

They had left the cave soon after dusk. Their mother had touched Tharak's chest and shown him an image before he left: dark trees, rising wind, and a still hand over a quiet heart. A message to stay aware, to move carefully, and to trust what he felt. She rarely used many gestures, but when she did, they lingered.

The elder remained behind with her, joints stiff with cold.

As they reached a rise in the trail, his father paused and turned. Without a sound, he dropped to all fours, smoothly and effortlessly navigating the mossy ground. Then he stood and shifted into a two-legged run. It was heavier, louder, more powerful. He turned and motioned for Tharak to copy.

Tharak followed, dropping to all fours. He moved quickly, faster than upright, more in tune with the forest floor. Then he rose and tried running upright again. Slower, less smooth, but strong. His father nodded. The lesson was simple. Use four legs for speed and stealth. Use two when you must face or defend.

They continued through the dark, Tharak keeping the lesson close.

Later, his father stopped again. He raised one hand and pointed. Veyla crouched low, already catching the scent. Tharak slowed and sank beside her. He caught the musk, the faint tang of animal sweat. A pig.

It stood just beyond a cluster of saplings, snout deep in soil, hunting for roots. It had not seen them. Had not heard them. Tharak watched as his father picked up a stone half the size of his forearm, tested the weight, then stood tall. With one breath, he threw.

The rock struck the side of the pig's skull with a crack like a broken branch. The animal dropped instantly, its legs folding beneath it.

Veyla gave a short hoot and rushed forward. Tharak followed, wide-eyed, as they checked the body. His father examined the strike point and nodded once.

Tharak was given the task of carrying it. He heaved it over his shoulder, the weight awkward but bearable. His steps were slow, careful on the uneven ground.

The path twisted back through the trees, up slopes slick with moss and down gullies where water still trickled from the last rain. They stopped once to drink, and Tharak leaned against a stump, catching his breath. His father said nothing.

Just waited.

When they reached the cave, the elder moved first, slow but steady, settling near the wall. Their mother followed, then their father, all three beginning the meal without ceremony.

Veyla joined them soon after, crouched close, hands already pulling at the meat. Tharak waited a moment longer, watching them, then knelt beside his sister and began to eat.

They ate together, tearing pieces of meat from the body with their hands and teeth. The heat of it warmed their bellies. No words were spoken, just the sound of flesh torn and chewed, the simple cadence of a shared meal.

Tonight, it was Tharak's turn to be the watcher. His father touched his arm once, a gesture of pride, and settled down with the others to sleep.

Tharak moved to the edge of the cave and crouched, his back straight, eyes scanning the trees beyond. The stars were high and cold, scattered across a wide sky. The land below was still. No wind. No movement.

He thought again of the hairless ones. The small one's face. The way her hands trembled. Her eyes, wide and wet. They looked delicate. Light. Their coverings hung off them like loose bark. They looked soft. Vulnerable. He had not sensed danger. Only difference.

The image stayed in his mind long after the wind shifted and the night deepened.

He sat quietly, his hand resting on the stone beneath him.

The land stretched below him, untouched and calm.

Tharak watched the tree line. The forest watched back. All was still in his world.

CHAPTER 5

Tharak woke to a quiet cave and the scent of absence. His family was already gone. He rose slowly, stretched aching limbs, and stepped outside. Their trail was fresh in the soil, and the wind carried them northeast. Toward the ridge.

He followed with care, slipping between trees, head low, footsteps silent. The forest held a strange hush. No birdsong. No movement from those that called the forest home.

By the time he reached the upper edge of the ridgeline, he spotted them farther down its slope, just above the valley floor. His father, mother, Veyla, and the elder were all crouched, still as stone, watching a herd of elk that grazed in the open field below. The sun cast a pale light over the slope, broken by patches of rock and thorny brush.

Tharak stood beside a tree, hidden. From his higher vantage point, he paused for a moment to watch them. There was a calm in their stance, a sense of belonging to this land.

A low vibration brushed his feet. A strange hum filled the air, rising with the wind.

His father stood and grunted loud enough for all to hear.

They moved instantly, springing into motion. Their feet pounded the rocky slope as they sprinted for the forest to the left of them.

Tharak flanked from above, keeping within the treeline, trying to follow their path. His chest grew tight. The humming grew louder, shifting into a deep mechanical roar. Wind tore through the branches. The treetops shuddered.

The mechanical bird burst over the ridge and swung low. Its form gleamed silver, limbs spinning so fast they blurred, slicing the sky with a shriek. It screamed as it flew.

Tharak's family had aimed for the treeline, but the bird dipped and slid sideways, cutting them off. The sound and force of it drove them off course, pushing them toward uneven ground, away from cover. It didn't strike them, didn't need to. It herded them.

The elder struggled with the slope, her pace faltering.

The first shot cracked through the morning air.

She flinched as it struck her in the back. Her arms flailed, and a sharp shriek tore from her throat. Another shot hit just below her shoulder. The third slammed into the back of her head. Her body folded. She tumbled forward, rolling down the ridge, limbs limp, blood streaking the rocks. She landed twisted at the base of the slope, unmoving.

Veyla halted, turning back toward the elder, her face stricken. Her father grunted again and shoved her forward. Her chest rose and fell fast, but she obeyed, breaking into a run.

Tharak moved along the treeline, heart racing, trying to stay with her. He whistled, sharp and high, willing her to turn.

She did.

Her eyes found his, full of fear and something else, knowing. He had never seen her afraid like that.

A shot cracked through the ridge. She jerked and stumbled. Another hit her side, and she screamed, falling hard. Her shoulder slammed into a boulder, and she crumpled onto her side, gasping as she began to crawl, dragging herself forward through blood and rocks.

The final shot hit her mid-spine.

Her body went rigid, then limp. She collapsed fully, her head lolling sideways, eyes fixed open toward the trees.

Tharak's whole body trembled. He had to bite down hard to stop the roar rising in his chest, had to dig his claws into the earth to keep from running to her.

His legs wobbled beneath him. His chest heaved, and his hands shook where they gripped the rocks beside him. His throat hurt.

Further down the slope, his parents kept running. They didn't look back.

The mechanical bird swung wide, then dropped fast again,

pushing air in violent waves as it came from above.

They had changed direction after Veyla fell, aiming for another patch of trees on the far side. But the bird dipped again, cutting them off.

Tharak's father turned, trying to shield his mate.

A shot hit him clean in the side of the neck. He staggered but stayed upright, choking out a guttural sound as his right hand clamped over the wound. The second tore through his ribs, driving the breath from him. The third struck his leg, and with a sharp grunt, he dropped to his knees.

His mate screamed and lunged to catch him, arms wrapping around his chest. The fourth shot hit her in the lungs, lifting her slightly off the ground before she collapsed on top of him, gasping, blood spilling from her mouth. As her body stilled, another shot cracked through the air and struck the back of her head.

They collapsed together, tangled in each other's limbs. The bird hovered a moment, drifting above them, then rose with sudden force and veered toward the west.

Stillness spread across the ridge.

Tharak remained where he was, crouched in shadow. As he watched them fall, he began to sway side to side, his body rocking with helpless rhythm. A thin, broken whine escaped his throat, high and soft, rising through clenched teeth. He dropped to his knees and pressed his forehead to the earth, eyes clenched shut. His breath came shallow and uneven. A low sound built deeper in his chest but never fully rose.

He got back onto his feet and paced beneath the trees, wearing a path between roots and brush, head low, shoulders shaking. Grief tangled in his limbs. He wanted to scream, to charge after the thing that had taken everything, but he stayed hidden.

Time passed. The sun rose higher.

The sound returned, slower now, pulsing above the treetops as the bird reappeared. It circled low and held steady in a hover over the ridge.

Four hairless ones descended from its belly, lowered by long cords that held them like dangling prey. Their legs were rigid and movements sharp. They landed near the bodies without a word. They wore bark-colored coverings that broke their shape, as if trying to become forest, and their thunder sticks glinted in the sun.

All four moved to the elder first, unrolling dark nets made from strange threads. Even with four of them, the body was heavy and unwieldy. Her limbs sagged as they pushed her into the folds of the net. Then they did the same with Veyla. Her hair dragged in the dirt as they wrapped her tightly, their movements slow and straining.

With hand signals, they called for lift. The machine began to rise. The elder and Veyla lifted into the sky, each suspended below the bird in wide, swaying nets. Arms hung down. Heads tipped back.

The first machine turned and drifted westward, their bodies swaying gently as they vanished between the trees.

Tharak did not move.

Another rumble came over the canopy.

A second bird arrived and held position above the slope.

Four more hairless ones descended. They carried the same thunder sticks, wore the same forest-colored coverings, and landed near the bodies of his father and mother.

All four moved to his father first. They rolled him slowly, pushing limbs into the folds of the black netting. They grunted and worked in rhythm, straining against the size and weight. His arms had stiffened. His mate's body was next. Her hair was soaked with blood, and it took effort to contain her limbs.

Both nets rose in turn. Their bodies hung low beneath the machine as it climbed, cords pulled tight, no sound but the blades above.

The four figures rose with them and vanished inside.

The second bird lifted and followed the path of the first.

Tharak stayed in the trees, buried in dirt and shadow. The ridge was empty again.

The forest was quiet. And nothing had ever felt more wrong.

CHAPTER 6

He woke hungry. Not the small hunger that nipped at the belly after a night of poor foraging. This was a deep pull that hollowed him out from throat to gut and made his hands curl against the dirt. Before he could always rely on his father for providing the food. Now there was only him, the damp ground, and the echo of the creek somewhere below the ridge.

He pushed himself upright and sniffed. Moss. Cold water. Rot from a fallen log. A raccoon had passed in the night, quick and nervous. A cougar had crossed the higher slope before dawn. Farther off, a family of deer. He could smell their bodies like soft warmth in the air, faint and teasing. His stomach clenched tight.

His father had taught him to listen first. To be still long enough for the forest to reveal itself. The big one would squat on his heels and barely breathe, eyes half-closed, head tilted as if the wind were speaking to him alone. Then he would point, and they would move. Slow. Silent. Certain.

Tharak tried to be certain now. He lowered himself, knees bent, arms loose, and waited with every muscle awake. A fly landed on his forearm. He did not shake it off. He counted the beats of his heart until the fly buzzed away.

There. A hoof clicked on stone. Not loud. Not near. But it shifted the map inside his head. He turned to the sound and inhaled slow and deep until he had it. Deer. More than one. Moving together. Down the slope, near the thin line of willow.

He moved.

Clumsy at first. He put his foot on a branch he hadn't seen, and it cracked under his weight. The sound made the birds lift all at once. He froze and tasted shame in his mouth, hot and bitter. His father would have cuffed him lightly for that and made him go back to the start and try again. There was no one to cuff him now, so he did it himself. A small tap to the back of his own head. A reminder. Be better. Be quiet.

He started over, this time feeling more than watching the ground. He placed his feet on the thick roots, the wet stones, the firm patches of moss. He moved beside a fern without touching it. He remembered his mother's hand guiding his wrist when he was small, teaching him to push leaves aside from underneath so they did not spring up for everyone to see.

When he reached the break in the trees, he saw them. Two grown and a young one, heads down, ears turning. The young one lifted its nose and sniffed, then returned to the grass. He could see the steam of their breath, thin and quick. He crouched and felt his breath match theirs. He did not know why he did that, only that it felt right. Shared rhythm. Shared heat.

He picked his path, looking for a line that would bring him around the side. The wind would not betray him if he kept to the low ground. The creek smell would help hide him. He pictured it the way his father taught him, like a marking in the dirt. He would go from this tree to that log to the hollow place behind the dark bush. Then he would wait. Then he would rush the smallest one. The muscles in his legs twitched with the thought, and he forced them still.

He made it to the log then to the bush. He took a breath and held it until his eyes watered. He waited. The young one lifted its head again and looked toward him, but not at him. Its ear flicked. A fly landed on its nose and it shook the fly away. The two grown ones moved, slow and trusting.

He burst from the brush too early.

His back foot slipped on a wet rock and kicked it. The rock clattered against another rock and both sounds hit the herd like a lash. The young one bolted. The grown ones followed. For a moment he was in the middle of them, arms out, fingers grabbing at air, legs pumping. He swiped at a flank that wasn't there anymore. He lunged and missed again.

One of the deer veered left and his body told him to go right. He fell forward, caught himself with his hands, and kept pushing. He did not think. He only ran. The smell of fear from the herd made his chest pound. A hoof slipped on dirt and a body skidded. He changed course without knowing how and slammed into something soft and fast and heavier than he thought it would be.

They both crashed hard. He rolled. He grabbed. He did not know what his hands had until it thrashed and kicked and almost tore free. He clamped down with everything in him, teeth bared, muscles screaming.

When it stopped moving, he realized he was holding only the back legs. The rest of it had twisted and broken in ways he hadn't intended. He stared at it a long time. He felt tired. Not proud. Not victorious. Just tired.

He dragged the carcass to the shelter of the trees and ate because his body demanded it. It was not graceful, and it was not the way he had been taught. He ate until the hollow place inside him closed and his limbs felt dense again. When he finished, he covered what remained with leaves and branches the way his mother used to. He was not sure why. The others were gone. There was no one to share.

When he stood, his legs shook. He looked down at himself and saw dirt and bits of green and blood. He went to the creek and washed until his skin felt like it belonged to him again. He sat on a flat rock and let the water chill the sore places.

He slept under a fallen fir that night. He dreamed of his father's hands, not rough or hard but steady. He dreamed of his mother's breath in the cold months, visible and close. He dreamed he was small again, and the world was big, not the other way around. He woke with his face wet and did not know if it was from rain or from himself. It did not matter.

The next day, hunger returned faster. Not as deep, but sharp enough to remind him that one kill was not enough to prove he could live. He stretched his back and tested his right ankle. It hurt from where he had slipped. He rolled it until the pain settled in the background, then stood and sniffed again.

No deer today. The air tasted different. Heavy with mud and the sweet rot of overturned soil. Pigs. He had watched his father bring them down many times. Quick. Certain. Sometimes with a fast rock, sometimes with a charge. He tried to remember how the big one had done it. Low. To the side. Not head on. Never head on. He nodded to himself. Low. To the side. He would charge.

He found them near a wallow, snouts deep, bodies pressed in clumps, eyes small and wary. He did not look at the biggest one. He kept his focus on a smaller shape near the edge. He did the map in his mind again. Tree, stump, hollow, rush. He moved. Slow at first. He placed his weight on the balls of his feet and felt the earth hold him. He uncurled his fingers and let them hang loose.

He almost made it clean. Then his stomach growled loudly and without thinking, he smacked his own belly with an annoyed grunt. The pigs' heads shot up. For a heartbeat, none of them moved. He froze with one foot lifted. The pig he had chosen blinked at him. He blinked back. It snorted once. He snorted too, out of reflex. The pig bolted. So did all the others.

He swore in a way only his kind did, a deep, low sound in the back of his throat that vibrated through his teeth. He launched after the slowest one. Every step sent mud up his shins. He slipped and caught himself on a tree, leaving a smear of wet earth behind. He grabbed a branch to swing himself forward, and it snapped. He went face-first into the wallow and came up sputtering, water in his nose and eyes stinging. As he shook himself off, he pictured his sister laughing at him, the way she used to when he did something foolish. The sound wasn't real, but it flickered in his mind. It made his chest ache. He blinked hard and pushed forward. The pigs were still running.

He caught up with the one he wanted only because it stumbled on a root. He did not make the same mistake as yesterday. He went low and to the side. He wrapped both arms around the midsection and lifted. It kicked and squealed and bit at his forearm. He grunted and squeezed. He felt the fight go out of it all at once. He set it down, chest heaving, and looked at it without moving for a long moment.

Afterward, he sat with his back to a tree. He looked at his hands. They were not the hands of the small one who watched and copied. They were his. Strong. Shaking a little. Covered in proof that he had done what he needed to do. He pressed them together, palm to palm, and felt the heat trapped between them.

A jay scolded from a branch above him and he looked up, squinting through leaves. The bird hopped twice, turned its head to look at him with one eye, and called again. Tharak responded with a huff. The jay fluffed its feathers, unimpressed, and flew away.

When the light began to fade, he carried what was left to a place only he knew, a part of the forest that still smelled faintly of his family. The scent was almost gone now, washed thin by rain and time, but he could still find it if he closed his eyes and let memory do the work. He did not eat there. He did not bleed there. He only sat. Sometimes he slept. That night, he sat and watched the shadow of his breath mix with the shadow of the trees.

He thought of the mechanical bird screeching through the sky, its spinning wings chopping the air. He remembered the panic in his family's eyes as they ran, not knowing where to go, their movements frantic and confused. His father had tried to shield them, but even he hadn't known what to do. Tharak had watched them scatter in fear, the sharp cracks echoing through the trees. He remembered his own cries, after they had been taken away by the hairless ones. He pressed his palms to the earth and let the cold seep in. It didn't take the memory away, but it dulled the edges. It dulled everything.

Before he slept, he whispered one of the sounds his mother made for comfort. A low humming that buzzed somewhere between chest and throat. It calmed the hair along his spine. It made his muscles loosen. It brought back the feeling of her comfort, soft and brief, and that was enough to let him close his eyes.

CHAPTER 7

Tharak never returned to the ridge. With each passing day, the weight of their loss settled deeper in his bones. He missed them more than he could understand. Their scent, once woven through every tree and trail, faded faster than he expected. The ridge no longer felt like home. It was only quiet now. Empty. And as the silence grew, so did the rage. Not toward the forest. Not toward the sky. But toward the hairless ones who had brought the end.

It started as a low thrum inside him. A bitter ember he couldn't extinguish. Each memory of their scent, their strange noises, their stinging tools, and fire, it fed the ember. And slowly, it began to burn.

So, he wandered.

He did not seek out others of his kind. If he smelled their presence, he changed direction. If he heard the echo of drums on bark or the distant calls that marked territory, he waited in silence or doubled back. The clans might have taken him in, or they might have challenged him. He didn't care to find out. He wasn't ready to speak. Not with hands. Not with breath. Not with memory.

What he carried inside could not be shown. Not the way the others understood.

He moved south, always south. At first he didn't know why. Something inside told him the land beyond was different. Warmer. Wilder. Farther from the machines. But deeper down, he knew it was because the hairless ones had taken his family and gone that way. The sky paths had led south. He had watched them vanish through the clouds.

So he followed that pull.

The forests changed as he moved. The pines near Lower Klamath Lake grew sparse, and the dry stretches between groves stretched longer with each season. Snow clung to the higher ridges longer than it used to. Springs came late, and creeks ran weaker.

He learned to dig roots from the cold ground and suck the moisture from the stalks. He cracked tree limbs for the grubs inside. The dead ones tasted like old bark and fat, but they kept him strong. He watched how the black bears dug under rocks for beetles. He watched how the ravens waited nearby, hoping for scraps. He watched, and he never stayed long.

During that first winter, he spent his nights tucked inside a hollow beneath a fallen cedar, wind howling over the rocks above. He wrapped his limbs tight and watched the dim light shift outside, marking time only by shadow and cold. The smell of snow and frozen bark became his world. Hunger became quiet. His muscles thinned. In sleep, he dreamed of his family: their faces, their sounds, the warmth of their breath beside him. Waking was harder each time.

But he lived.

By the second year, he crossed lowland swamps where the ground shifted beneath his feet. Willow roots snagged his legs, and snakes watched him from the water, still and coiled. He stepped on one and it struck at his ankle, but the fangs slid harmlessly across his matted hair and thick skin. The pain was no more than a pinch. He crushed it with a rock and chewed the meat, which tasted of mud and rot.

Some time in the third year, he found a pile of feathers and blood, a hawk, torn apart. He didn't know what had killed it, but the air smelled wrong. Too much copper. No predator left meat untouched unless something else had already claimed it.

He kept moving.

In the fourth year, he climbed the shoulders of Mount Shasta, though he never reached the peak. The wind up high stung his eyes, and the snow hadn't melted even when the valleys below were green. From that height, he looked back once toward the lake of his birth, but he saw nothing. No birds. No movement.

The girl's face returned to his mind, blonde hair, pale skin, eyes wide with fear. He remembered how she had screamed, how her voice had echoed.

And how, not long after, only two sun sleeps later, the sky

machines had come.

He knew it was connected. Somehow, that child had summoned the end of his family.

Every time he passed the edge of a clearing or heard voices in the distance, he thought of her. Every time the wind carried the scent of human fire, he remembered the screams.

In the sixth year, he had crossed into the forests that clung to the edge of California. The trees there were strange. Some stood wide enough that he could not wrap both arms around their base. The bark peeled in strips. The ferns grew tall and thick. In the early mornings, the mist hung so low he could barely see his feet.

He began to move only at dusk or just before dawn.

The prey animals here were cautious. The deer with black-tipped tails moved in small groups, snorting and stamping even before he crept within reach. He learned to wait high in the trees, watching them pass below. Sometimes he dropped onto their backs, snapping necks in a single twist. Other times he let them go, too tired to chase.

More often, he fished.

The rivers here held trout in the spring and fall. He found the shallow spots where they darted between stones, backs flashing silver in the current. He waited knee-deep, patient, until one brushed his leg. Then he struck.

He tore into the meat, blood staining his chest, the bones cracking between his teeth. It made him feel strong. It made him forget.

In the seventh year, one summer afternoon, he smelled something strange riding the wind. It stung his nose and made the back of his throat itch. The scent grew heavier, thicker, until the trees themselves began to hiss. The air shimmered. Creatures ran from the hills, rabbits, deer, even black bears, not with fear, but with desperation.

He ran too.

The red-breath swept the forest behind him. Its smoke curled like claws around the trunks. Heat pulsed through the ferns. Leaves turned black and crumbled. The ground itself seemed to groan.

He ran until his legs failed, then crawled into a stream and let the water cover him.

In the morning, when the smoke thinned, and the heat began to fade, he rose from the shallows, aching and cold. The forest he knew was silent. Trees still stood, but their limbs were blackened and bare. The ferns were gone. Birds did not sing.

He walked for hours through the scorched valley. Beneath the ash, he found the curled remains of deer, foxes, snakes, and birds. All turned to bone and dust.

A heaviness settled in his chest. These were not his clan,

but they were his kin. The forest had always spoken to him in scent and shadow, in hunger and shelter. Now it was quiet.

And he was alone again.

In the eighth year, he came upon a small clearing where two hairless males had made camp.

He had smelled them first: sweat, heat, the bitter stink of something unnatural, and the sour trail of their refuse. Shiny skins crumpled and scattered like shed bark. A small heat-pile burned at the center of their space, coughing gray breath into the branches above. The scent clawed at his memory. The red-breath had taken too much. It had blackened his forest, silenced the animals, and left nothing but bones. His mouth tightened. His nose curled. His breath slowed.

Their voices scraped the stillness, loud and careless.

They had no beasts. No watchers. They didn't know what moved just beyond the dark.

Tharak crouched low, hidden behind fern and stone.

They laughed. One threw a hollow thing that clanked against another. The other raised a glinting piece to his mouth and drank from it, then tossed it aside with no thought. Their movements were clumsy. Their sounds louder than they needed to be. Wrong in every way.

Tharak's throat rumbled. He could feel the rage inside him build.

He moved closer.

He snapped a twig. On purpose.

One of the males straightened, peering toward the trees.

"Did you hear that?"

The other one made a noise like a grunt and said, "Probably a raccoon."

Tharak stepped again, closer to the edge of their glow. The heat-pile crackled near them. The taller one's face changed. He reached toward his side but did not draw the thunder stick.

Tharak growled. Deep and low.

Now both of them were standing. Their eyes locked on the trees. One backed away.

"What the fuck is that?"

He showed himself.

He stood at the edge of the firelight, towering and still, his massive form half-swallowed by shadow. For a moment, no one moved. No one breathed. He didn't look like a man, or a bear, or anything they knew. His skin was the color of charcoal, rough like cracked leather. His hair hung in thick, damp strands, tangled with leaves and clumps of earth. His brow was heavy, his eyes sunken and black, too deep to see anything human inside them. The way he stared, unblinking and unshaken, felt colder than the air. The firelight danced along his chest and arms, picking out details that made no sense. Long limbs. Massive hands. Muscles built for tearing. He looked like something pulled from the darkest part of the mind, a shape you forget after a nightmare but still fear when the lights go out. And he was real. Standing right there. Staring right at them.

The two hairless stared in disbelief.

One of them fumbled with a light-stone, casting it toward him. It flashed across his chest.

Tharak roared.

The sound rolled through the clearing like a boulder down a cliff, shaking the leaves from the branches.

They bolted.

Not for their tools. Not for their coverings. One tripped on his bedding skin and crashed to the ground, scrambling up again with his hands clawing at the dirt.

But they didn't flee into the woods.

They sprinted for the large metal beast, crouched low among the trees. The second one reached it first, flung open a side flap, and shouted. The other dove in just behind him.

The beast screamed to life, spitting smoke from its tail. It groaned, then rolled backward, crunching over twigs and roots. A bright light flared. The noise was sharp and unnatural. The stench that followed was worse, hot stone, scorched metal, and something acrid that didn't belong in the forest.

Tharak lunged forward and struck the back of the creature with an open palm. The surface was hard and cold, not like bone or bark, and it rang out beneath his hand with a hollow thud. It shuddered and threw dirt behind it as it turned, then fled down the trail, growling louder as it gained speed, vanishing into the dark.

He stood in the clearing.

The heat-pile hissed low in the torn grass. Their cast-off tools lay scattered. The stink of them still clung to the ferns.

He had meant to end them.

But he was too slow, and they had escaped.

Tharak turned without a sound and slipped back into the forest. The dark welcomed him.

Not long after the two hairless males had fled their camp, Tharak came upon a new scent in the forest. It was not one or two. It was many. The air near the southern hills stung his nose, heavy with rot and bitter smoke. The trees ahead moaned in the wind, even though there was no storm.

He followed the sound.

By mid-afternoon, he crouched in the branches of a tall pine, still as bark, staring down at a clearing that had not existed days before. Trees lay broken and scattered, torn from the ground and stripped of their limbs. Their trunks were dragged into stacks. Their roots reached skyward like the dead frozen in place.

Guttural machines rested among the ruin, their arms locked and teeth stained with bark and sap. One still moved. It hissed and spun and chewed, coughing out shards from its metal belly.

Hairless ones walked between the fallen, marking trunks, making sharp noises and strange calls that rose over each other. One threw aside an empty container that glinted in the grass.

Tharak's fingers dug into the wood beneath him.

He stayed as the day faded. None of them looked toward the trees. Their eyes did not search the shadows.

When the sun began to fall, most climbed into a long metal beast that groaned and rolled away, leaving deep scars in the ground. But one hairless one stayed behind. A smaller one with thin arms and a bright round cover on his head. He crouched beside one of the broken machines, mumbling, kicking at the wheel.

The others shouted from the carrier.

He waved them off and stayed.

The carrier left. The forest grew quiet again.

Tharak watched.

The hairless one circled the edge of the clearing, shining a small glowing stone into the trees, talking to himself. He pulled a stick from his belt and placed it between his lips. Smoke rose. The scent was bitter, unnatural.

He sat on one of the dead trunks and stared into the growing dark.

Then he turned toward the trees.

Tharak had not moved.

Still, the hairless one squinted.

A gust stirred the branches above. One of the timber stacks groaned, creaking under its own weight.

The hairless one stood quickly and raised the glowing stone, sweeping it back and forth.

"Hello?" he called.

Tharak stepped from the brush behind him.

Not fast. Not loud.

The hairless one turned at the sound.

Tharak struck with one arm across the throat, knocking him backward. The hairless one hit the ground hard, wheezing, his limbs jerking as he tried to scramble away. His light clattered from his hand and went dark.

Tharak moved forward and pressed a foot into the hairless one's side, pinning him. He reached down, gripped the strange bright covering, and dragged him toward the edge of the clearing.

He did not strike again.

Not yet.

He wanted the hairless one to feel it.

To feel the fear that his mother must have felt.

That Veyla had carried in her eyes before they dimmed.

That his father must have swallowed in silence to protect them.

The hairless one gasped and struggled, eyes wide.

Tharak watched.

Then he rolled the body over, placed a hand on the chest, and pressed until something deep inside gave way. The last breath escaped without a sound.

He lifted the body and carried it back into the clearing.

The machines loomed above the stumps like dead giants frozen mid-meal.

He chose one of them.

A tall one with a long, jointed arm, and a cage where the hairless ones sat to command it. Tharak climbed the wheel and lifted the body, wedging it into the seat. The head lolled forward, chin to chest, arms limp at the sides. The blood from his broken chest had soaked into his shirt, dark and sticky.

Tharak stepped down and looked up at the figure now slumped in the machine.

Let them see.

He vanished into the trees without a sound.

By the ninth year, his body had grown larger. He now stood over eight feet tall, his shoulders thick with strength earned by hunger and hard ground. His legs carried him farther without rest. His stride could cover a riverbank in seconds.

Over the years, his hair had grown coarse and matted, tangled with leaf and bramble. He had not cared enough to keep it otherwise, and he had no partner to help clean or groom him the way his mother or sister once had.

His face bore a long, pale scar from a fight with a black bear he had surprised at a carcass. The claw had torn down from cheek to jaw, and the wound had healed unevenly, pulling the corner of his mouth into a permanent slant that gave his expression a twisted, silent snarl.

But the weight in his chest had not changed.

He still saw their faces.

He still heard the bird.

When he passed the edges of human towns, he crouched beneath bridges or waited in culverts while their machines passed overhead. Their lights were too bright. Their noise too constant.

They did not belong in the forest.

But they came anyway.

He watched them leave trash along trails. Watched them build paths with gravel. Watched them cut trees that had stood for longer than he had been alive.

He hated them.

And always, the image returned. The blonde-haired girl. Small and soft. Her scream had reached farther than any sound he had ever heard. He did not know her name, but he remembered her face. He remembered the shape of her eyes. The way she had turned when her father called her back. That glance, full of confusion.

That face lived behind his eyes now.

By the tenth year, he had reached the thick forests just north of a wide stretch of broken land the hairless ones called a town. He had followed the rivers south, always choosing the high paths, away from roads. The forests near Redding grew hot in summer, full of biting insects and wild pigs that tore at the roots. He slept in dry creek beds and ate whatever he could find.

There were other Sasquatch nearby. He smelled them. Sometimes, late at night, he heard their voices carried on the wind. Low calls. Throat sounds. Echoes of language he once used.

He never approached.

The first time, they found him instead.

A young male stepped onto the trail below his resting place, shoulders broad but movements uncertain. Behind him, two others waited, older, more cautious. Their scent was clean, their posture balanced. They said nothing at first, only watched.

Tharak dropped down from the rocks, slow and steady. He made no sound.

The young male grunted and raised his palm, signaling caution, not challenge. One of the elders motioned toward the trees, then thumped his chest once, firm and clear. An invitation.

Tharak didn't answer.

They repeated the gesture. Come with us. Join. Belong.

Tharak grunted low and scraped a wide circle in the dirt with his foot. Then he stepped back, raised one arm, and swept it outward. No.

The wind shifted between them. No one moved.

The younger one growled softly, confused. The elders gave no further gesture. Tharak turned and walked away.

They did not follow.

After that, he stayed in the dark. The shadows felt more like home than anything else.

He stopped in a narrow canyon not far from a fast river. A cave there opened in the rock just wide enough for his shoulders. It was dry, and the moss at the entrance stayed green even when the heat came. He drank from the spring that bubbled below and ate lizards when the rabbits disappeared. When the ache in his belly became too much to ignore, he hunted deer and wild pigs, dragging their bodies back to the cave and feeding until the hunger settled.

Even then, he never let himself sleep too deeply.

He still dreamed of the rotors.

Of the nets.

Of Veyla's eyes just before they went still.

Of the tree line they had never reached.

He never wept. But he remembered. And his heart burned with rage.

CHAPTER 8

In 1987, Senator Walter Granger stepped off the tarmac and made a call. Not a report. Not a request. A directive. Within forty-eight hours, four creatures were killed by helicopter teams near Upper Klamath Lake. Their bodies vanished without a trace.

He had seen three of them. They had stared him down without fear. One of them had looked into his daughter's eyes. They made him feel helpless. Exposed. Small.

That feeling stayed with him.

Back in Washington, he returned to his schedule. Floor votes. Hearings. Cameras. But everything else took second place. What mattered now was control. Quiet control.

Using his position as Oregon's senior senator, he diverted funds into rural emergency preparedness programs, forestry initiatives, and wildlife containment contracts. He pulled favors from state offices. He contacted former military contractors and private security groups.

He formed a unit.

Sentinel Branch.

It operated only in Oregon, under classified environmental oversight. No public documents. No official designations. Its work was labeled as fire risk assessment and ecological disruption response.

Its real purpose was eradication.

He hired a former intelligence officer to track movements in wilderness zones. Brought in contractors with combat experience. Equipped them with thermal optics, suppressed weapons, containment gear, and the authority to kill.

Sentinel Branch began in the Cascades. Then spread through the central range. Then into the dense forests near the state border. Teams rotated through hot zones. They moved quietly, operated without press, and reported directly to Walter's private office.

Every mission was recorded only as a logistical expenditure.

Every confirmed kill marked progress.

Walter didn't want research. He didn't want to study them. He wanted them gone. Not relocated. Not tagged. Gone.

He believed they were spreading. He saw them as a perversion of nature. And he believed no one else had the nerve to do what had to be done.

The creatures had made him feel powerless. He built Sentinel to take that power back.

Each operation reinforced his purpose. Every silenced report, every recovered sample, every erased footprint, proof that he had turned fear into control.

Walter Granger no longer saw the forest as protected land. He saw it as a battlefield. And in his mind, the outcome was already decided.

They had let him live. That had been their mistake.

Five years after his encounter, Walter Granger began showing signs of dementia. As the condition worsened, he forgot names, dates, and entire chapters of his life. But the one thing he never forgot were the faces of the creatures at Upper Klamath Lake. He didn't remember what they were called, only the way they looked at him. Long after everything else faded, they stayed with him. In sleep, they returned more vivid than memory, chasing him through the forest, hunting him down. He woke often, drenched in sweat, breathless and afraid, unable to explain why.

The mind that had once hunted them now belonged to them.

CHAPTER 9

-2002-

Diana Beretti had never liked the way the woods fell silent at dusk. It wasn't just the fading light, but how the wind slowed and the small animals seemed to vanish. She had grown up learning to read those silences. Her grandmother used to say the watchers came when the hush settled in. You didn't hear them arrive. You felt it.

She had felt it again that evening. A quiet anxiety curled in her chest.

Their home in Blackridge sat a few miles out of town, nestled against a ridge thick with pine and cedar. It was peaceful and quiet, especially in the mornings when sunlight touched the trees and the birds began to stir. Their closest neighbors lived about half a mile away, a kind older couple with grown children who rarely visited.

The road leading to the house was narrow and cracked, paved years ago and haphazardly patched whenever the county remembered it. Just enough to keep traffic light and strangers few.

She had loved the isolation for years. But after their daughter Nicole began to walk and wander, the silence that once soothed her began to stir a quiet panic.

Daniel was home, for once, and that helped. Her husband of sixteen years had been in the military since they were both twenty. His presence made her feel grounded again, but his absence had shaped most of their life together. He had grown quieter over the years. Still strong and affectionate with Nicole, still quick to smile, but often elsewhere in his mind. She never asked what he saw when he went quiet, and he never said. That was the rhythm they had fallen into long ago.

When Diana wasn't looking after Nicole or tending the home, she worked with her hands. She had learned knife-making from her maternal uncle, a quiet man with strong fingers and old knowledge. They had converted the attached garage into a small workshop where Diana shaped steel and carved antler handles, wrapping them in sinew or leather. She sold the finished knives at a Native-owned store in town, which brought in a little extra money and helped keep her hands busy. Nicole often spent hours beside her mother in that space, watching closely, asking questions, sometimes sanding the handles smooth. Diana never said it aloud, but she found comfort in that room, in the steady flow of the work, the scent of forged steel and rawhide, and the deep satisfaction that came from honest effort and purpose.

Nicole didn't notice the space between her parents. At twelve, nearly thirteen, she was too full of movement and curiosity to see what stayed still. She ran through the woods like they were hers by birthright, always barefoot when she thought she could get away with it, always climbing trees or balancing on logs across creek beds. She had her father's confidence, her mother's intuition, and her uncle's restless spirit.

Benjamin, Daniel's younger brother, had helped raise Nicole in ways that mattered. She adored him. He took her out into the wilds for whole afternoons, and sometimes for days at a time, camping deep in the backcountry where there was no signal and no one else around. He taught her how to fish, hunt, track, build shelters, and move without sound. He showed her how to live off the land, how to read weather in the leaves, how to light a fire in the rain, and how to tell which berries could be eaten and which could kill you. It wasn't just the usual family outings. He made her capable. Between him and Daniel, Nicole had learned how to load and fire a rifle before she was eight, how to handle a bow properly, and how to carry a blade without fear. She wasn't reckless. She just understood that danger existed and believed she could meet it.

She loved sports, especially anything that tested her endurance or balance. Running through uneven terrain, scrambling over rock faces just to see what was on the other side. She didn't care if her hands got cut or if her boots tore on the ridge trail. The wild didn't scare her. It called to her.

And it worried Diana.

Because some things out there didn't care how skilled you

were. Some things were old, quiet, and uninterested in fairness.

The watchers weren't new. They had been part of Diana's life since she was a child. Where she grew up, it wasn't unusual to see one at the tree line or hear movement just beyond the light. People didn't panic. But they were always cautious. Her grandmother told stories of tall, silent ones with wide shoulders and knowing eyes. You weren't supposed to name them aloud, and you never gave them yours. They weren't spirits or protectors, not really. Just watchers. Observers of the human world, curious but unpredictable. There were stories passed quietly from porch to firepit, about people who wandered too far into the forest and were never seen again. The watchers kept their distance until they didn't.

Daniel had laughed when Diana first told him about the watchers. But after the night something slapped the side of their house hard enough to rattle the windows, his tone shifted.

Nicole was three the first time they heard the knocks. It was late. Three dull thuds against the wall of the bedroom. Diana pulled Nicole closer to her in bed, holding her tight as she stared toward the window, her breath locked in her throat. There were no more knocks that night, but the feeling that followed crept into the bones of the house and stayed.

Things escalated slowly after that. Pinecones were left in odd piles on the steps. Stones were tossed at the back door, never to break anything, just to announce presence. They heard pacing along the edges of the clearing, heavy but precise.

Once, something ran the length of the roof while Nicole slept. Another time, Daniel found the lid of their garbage can placed upright thirty feet away, not spilled, just moved.

Some nights, long after midnight, they heard sounds that didn't belong. Sharp cracks, like wood striking wood. Long, low howls that drifted across the ridge and didn't match any known animal. There were calls that mimicked owls but were slightly off, as if something had heard them once and tried to repeat them without understanding the tone. The sounds came from different distances. Sometimes close. Sometimes far. But always from the woods.

Over time, Diana began to notice something unsettling. The watchers weren't just present near the house. They always seemed more interested in Nicole than anyone else. Even when Daniel or Ben were outside, even when Diana herself stood in full view, their focus remained fixed on the girl.

It started subtly with small gifts being left.

Shiny things. Smooth, bright pebbles or rocks. A few marbles, too perfect to have come from the woods, appeared one morning directly beneath Nicole's window. Diana found a tarnished brass button there too, placed just beneath the sill in the grass. Once, there was an old broken doll with matted hair and one missing eye, its fabric faded and damp from the morning dew. None of the items belonged to them.

Diana gathered them and placed them in a bag.

Later that evening, she mentioned it to Daniel. He listened while cleaning his rifle, nodding without interruption.

"I don't like it," she had said. "It's like they're choosing her."

He had paused, looked up, and said quietly, "We'll just have to keep an extra eye on here. But I wouldn't worry too much. She's smart. She knows how to take care of herself."

Diana hadn't disagreed. But the unease stayed with her.

Because being smart didn't mean you couldn't be watched.

And being watched didn't mean you were safe.

The watchers never approached Nicole, but they did study her. They watched from the tree line or from behind low ridges. And Nicole watched them back. Not frightened. Not dismissive. Just curious. She stared as if they were animals she hadn't seen before, like something worth understanding. She had a way of being still that Diana didn't expect from a child. No waving or shouting. Just focused attention.

That morning, Diana stood barefoot on the porch with a cup of coffee, letting her soles press into the cool grain of the boards. The fog drifted low over the grass, thick as wool, and the birds hadn't yet started. The silence pulled at her. She stepped off the porch and let her feet sink into the damp earth, grounding herself the way her grandmother had taught her. Something had passed through during the night. Something that left the world just a little too still in its wake.

Nicole burst through the door not long after, laces half-tied, flannel askew, and a grin already on her face.

"Going to the creek!"

"Take your whistle."

She groaned, rolled her eyes, grabbed the orange whistle from the hook beside the door, and jogged off into the trees.

Daniel stood in the kitchen, frying eggs and flipping them one-handed. He didn't ask where she was going. He trusted her.

So did Diana, most of the time.

That afternoon, she found a broken maple branch just beyond the edge of the grass. It hadn't fallen. It had been twisted clean and left at an angle across a stone, like it had been placed. A marker. She rested her fingers on the tear in the wood and waited. The sensation it left behind was cold and heavy.

Inside, Daniel was on the phone. Something official. Something quiet and clipped. He didn't say it, but she knew. He'd be gone again soon.

That night, the sky cleared. Nicole was already asleep, curled into her blanket with the whistle on the nightstand beside her. Daniel was in the shower.

Diana walked past the living room window, then paused, something catching on the periphery of her vision. She stepped back and looked out.

A shape stood at the edge of the clearing. Taller than anything they had seen before. He was clearly male, with shoulders wider than a doorway and arms that hung long and motionless. He didn't shift his weight. He didn't move at all.

His eyes were not the usual amber.

They were red.

Not glowing. But vivid. Intense. Focused.

Diana stayed where she was, meeting his stare through the glass.

He tilted his head slightly, not like an animal, but like something confused or intrigued. Not aggressive. Just still.

She didn't call for Daniel. She didn't move away.

She watched until he stepped backward into the trees and vanished into the dark.

Then she whispered to herself, "That one's not like the others."

CHAPTER 10

The forest around the creek stilled as the scent of a hairless one drifted through the trees.

Tharak moved with silence shaped by years of solitude. Every step was intentional. Every shift of his weight was absorbed by instinct. He followed no trail. He didn't need one. His feet found the quietest places, worn only by the passing of prey and the pull of the wind.

The scent was not sharp like fear. It was not old. It was fresh, warm, and strange.

He crouched low beside a cluster of ferns, his arms bent, and hands spread wide across the moss. The creek curved through the trees just ahead, and beyond its bend, light spilled through the canopy in a broken pattern.

Then he saw her.

A young female hairless one knelt at the water's edge, her hand dipping into the current. Yellow hair spilled over her shoulders. It caught the sun and shimmered like something alive. She was small, narrow-limbed, with skin like pale bark and eyes the color of glacial ice. She was not afraid. She didn't know he was there.

Tharak did not move.

She crouched, watching a small fish zip by in the water, then smiled. The sound she made was soft, almost like a purr, and it curled beneath his ribs in a way he didn't expect. It was similar to a sound his sister used to make when she found something curious.

But it wasn't his sister crouching at the creek.

And it wasn't the yellow-haired hairless one from the days before everything ended. But she looked the same.

Before the sky machines. Before the thunder sticks.

Before the smell of his family torn open and rolled into nets.

Tharak's jaw tightened, his molars grinding together with slow, steady force. He dropped lower into the brush, his fingers splayed in the dirt. He remembered the way Veyla had screamed when the noise began. He remembered the sound of the elder's bones snapping. His father's body falling. His mother's breath stopping. The girl before this one had stared at him with eyes wide and mouth open screaming before the male hairless one pulled her away and raised a thunder stick.

And now this one.

This one with the same yellow hair and the same wide eyes, blue like the morning sky above the high ridges. She moved the same way. Looked at the world with the same wonder. Like nothing had ever tried to kill her. Like the trees were her home.

He hated that about her.

She didn't know what it was like to have your whole family taken from you.

But he couldn't stop watching.

She leaned closer to the water. A leaf floated past her hand and she chased it with her fingertips. Her boots were wet, her hair tangled at the ends. She wasn't graceful, but she was un-afraid. That made her dangerous.

Hairless ones always took what they feared. They destroyed what they couldn't control. This girl should have felt wrong in this place. But she didn't. She belonged here more than most of them. And that confused him.

He crouched deeper, breath slow and steady. The scent of the creek mixed with her own. Her skin, her hair, the salt from where she had likely run or climbed before she arrived here. She smelled alive in a way that made his memory ache.

He should have left.

He should have turned away.

But instead, he watched her like she was a puzzle missing one stone. Not prey. Not enemy. Not quite anything he had words for.

Just a shape that reminded him of the worst day of his life.

His claws pressed against the earth. He could have stepped into view. She would have screamed. She would have run. She would have told the others. And maybe they would have come again with machines and metal and noise.

But he didn't.

He stayed in the shadowed brush and burned in silence.

She began to hum softly. A song with no shape, just drifting sounds and slow breath. Her voice didn't match the face in his memory, but it stuck to him all the same.

A crow landed on a low branch above her and squawked twice, loud and sharp. The sound made her pause. She looked up, then turned away from the creek, brushing her hands on her pants.

When she stood, he stayed low and followed from the trees.

She moved through the undergrowth without looking back.

He tracked her step for step, silent and hidden, weaving through shadow and root. She paused once to tie a bootlace, then continued up the trail that led toward the open clearing beyond the ridge.

She stopped suddenly.

He froze.

She turned her head and scanned the woods behind her,

brows drawing together. Her gaze passed across the trees, narrowed slightly, then softened. After a moment, she exhaled and kept walking.

He stayed just far enough behind.

The sun shifted. The light deepened. She reached the edge of the trees and crossed the clearing toward the house that sat tucked against the slope.

Tharak lingered at the edge of the woods, chest rising and falling, watching her walk through the door and disappear inside.

Only then did he turn away.

CHAPTER 11

The morning light filtered through the kitchen windows in long, dusty bands. Diana stood at the sink, rinsing blueberries for breakfast, watching a pair of finches hop along the porch railing. The birds were loud this morning, almost too loud, as if they were trying to fill a silence that had settled inside her since last night.

Daniel entered from the hallway, pulling a flannel shirt over his shoulders. His hair was still damp from the shower, and his boots scuffed across the old wooden floor as he crossed to the table. He poured himself a cup of coffee, then sat down with a groan that seemed to echo in the quiet room.

She didn't turn right away. "You're up early," she said.

He took a sip and nodded. "Couldn't sleep. Too much on my mind."

Diana glanced at him over her shoulder. "You going to tell me what it is, or should I guess?"

He hesitated before answering. "Orders came in yesterday. I'm leaving on the 28th."

She put the bowl of blueberries down a little harder than she meant to. The splash of water spread across the counter, unnoticed. "That soon?"

"Yeah."

Diana leaned against the counter, arms crossed over her chest. "Why hadn't you told me?"

He looked down into his mug. "I didn't want to ruin the morning."

She studied him for a long moment. "That would imply the morning wasn't already on edge."

He met her eyes, brow creasing.

She sighed and pushed away from the counter. "I saw something last night."

His posture stiffened, just slightly. "What kind of something?"

"One of them."

He didn't ask what she meant. "Where?"

"By the old garden bed."

Daniel sat forward. "How close?"

"Thirty yards. Maybe less. He didn't move. Just stood there. Watching."

He rubbed his jaw. "Was it the older one?"

She shook her head. "No. This one was taller. Broad through the shoulders. And his eyes…"

"What about them?"

"They were red."

Daniel didn't say anything at first. He looked toward the window like he might spot something now. "Red eyes," he repeated, quietly.

"I've never seen one like that before," she said, staring out the kitchen window, her arms wrapped around herself. "The others always seemed curious, maybe a little bold. But this one didn't blink. He didn't leave when I noticed him. Just stared right back at me.

His fingers tightened around the coffee mug.

"I don't like it," she said. "Something about this one feels different."

He nodded once, slowly. "I'll put up more motion sensor lights. Maybe some around the shed and the back trail. I can swing by the hardware store after breakfast and pick up whatever I need."

Diana turned to face him. "Make sure they are up today. Please."

"I will."

The back door creaked open before Diana could say anything else. Nicole stepped inside, a small handful of blueberries cupped in one palm. Her braid was messy, her shoes wet with dew, and she wore a Pat Benatar shirt with shorts.

Diana's eyes narrowed. "Where have you been?"

Nicole shrugged. "Just down by the creek."

Worry showed on Diana's face. "I don't want you going out there alone anymore. Especially that far from the house."

"Why?" Nicole asked, brows drawing together.

Diana hesitated. Her eyes flicked to Daniel, then back to Nicole. "Just do as I ask. Please."

Nicole frowned, but nodded. "Fine."

She walked to the fridge and opened it, pulling out the orange juice. Daniel gave her a small smile that didn't quite reach his eyes. "Morning, kiddo."

"Morning, Dad," she mumbled, pouring a glass and leaning against the counter as she drank. Her gaze moved between them. "You two look serious."

"Just talking about some house stuff," Daniel said.

"Like what?"

"Lights," Diana said. "Your dad's going to put up some new ones around the yard."

"Because of the watchers?"

Daniel glanced at her. "You've seen them again?"

"Not really. Just heard stuff. Knocked over the garbage can again two nights ago." She shrugged. "No big deal."

Diana exchanged a glance with Daniel. He said nothing.

Nicole took another drink, then set the glass down. "Hey, if you're going into town, can I come?"

Daniel looked at her. "You want to come to the hardware store?"

"I want to get more sketch pads. I'm out." She pointed toward the table where her last pad lay open, half-filled with penciled shapes and shadows of animals and trees.

He nodded. "Alright. Let me get my wallet and we'll head out in a few."

Nicole smiled and slipped out of the kitchen. Diana waited until she was gone before speaking again.

"You should tell Ben about the one with red eyes," she said quietly. "If something happens while you're gone, I want him to be paying close attention."

Daniel stood and kissed her temple. "I'll talk to him tonight."

She nodded and turned back to the sink, running water over the blueberries again, even though they were already clean. "I've got a bad feeling, Dan. This one isn't like the others."

"I believe you."

CHAPTER 12

Rain ticked gently against the roof while the glow of the television flickered across the living room walls. Diana sat curled into one corner of the couch, a blanket pulled across her lap, her eyes fixed on the screen. Nicole lay stretched across the rug with a bowl of popcorn balanced on her stomach, quoting lines from *The Goonies* as they came.

"Hey you guuuuys," she shouted along with the movie, laughing as the characters stumbled through the tunnel.

Diana shook her head and smiled. "I swear, I don't know how that tape still works. You've watched it so many times, it should be nothing but static by now."

"I love it. It's gonna be a classic one day, Mom. You'll see."

The room felt warm and easy for the first time all week. The storm outside was light, barely enough to bring the chill through the windows. Daniel's absence weighed on Diana, but these small moments, blankets, popcorn, and a shared movie, were the pieces she held together.

A sudden sound shattered it.

A single smack against the side of the house, deep and violent, struck like an open hand slamming against the wall. The entire living room jolted. The bookshelf rattled, and a framed photo tipped forward, landing flat on the hardwood with a soft crack.

Nicole shot upright, eyes wide.

Diana froze.

They looked at each other.

Diana raised her eyebrows and gave Nicole a small, tight-lipped look. The one that said, without speaking, you know what that was.

Nicole gave the faintest nod, her face serious for once.

Diana reached slowly for the remote, adjusted the volume just slightly lower, not off. She didn't want it to go silent. She didn't want whatever was out there to know they were listening.

The movie kept playing.

Nicole leaned back, eyes flicking between the screen and the front window. Diana tried to match her ease, but her muscles remained tight, shoulders drawn, breath shallow.

Minutes passed.

From the far side of the house came a new sound.

Tapping.

One tap. Then another. And another. Not random. Not hurried. A slow, methodical rhythm, like fingers drumming as their owner walked.

The motion sensor light outside the kitchen window flared on.

Nicole turned to look but didn't see anything.

Diana didn't move.

The tapping crept along the wall, growing slightly louder as it approached the front of the house. A second light came on, this one outside the living room window, casting a faint glow that slipped through the narrow gaps at the sides of the blinds. Both of them followed the sound with their eyes, tracking it from one wall to the next.

Neither of them breathed.

The blinds were down. They always were after sunset. Diana had learned that lesson years ago, the hard way. Seeing a face pressed to the glass, massive, broad, and impossibly close, had changed how she lived. Since then, the blinds came down with the dusk. Every night. Without fail.

They waited.

A deep growl rose up from the other side of the glass. It started low, too low to register as sound at first. Just pressure. It climbed slowly, growing stronger, vibrating through the couch, the floor, the walls. It filled the room and their chests, shaking the frames of the windows, settling into their ribs like something physical. It lasted at least thirty seconds, an unbroken rumble that could only come from a creature with lungs the size of barrels.

Diana sat still, her heartbeat so loud she was sure it could be heard. She felt the sound more than she heard it. She felt it in her jaw, behind her eyes, through her spine.

Slowly, quietly, she got up and crossed the room. She sat beside Nicole and wrapped an arm around her shoulders, pulling her close without a word.

It stopped.

Silence returned.

The air in the room felt thick and still.

Diana swallowed hard. "We're okay," she whispered.

"I know," Nicole said without looking away from the television.

Diana glanced at her daughter and felt something twist deep in her chest. Nicole didn't react like most people would, not even close. She wasn't frozen or panicked. Her hands weren't shaking. She hadn't cried out or run. Maybe she was scared on the inside and just hiding it well. Or maybe she wasn't scared at all. She just took it in, accepted it, like she'd been expecting it somehow.

The movie kept playing. Sloth yelled from the pirate ship. Mouth was translating the map wrong again. Nicole chuckled like nothing had happened.

Diana slowly stood and walked to the hallway, checking the locks on the back door, the front, the kitchen door. All secure. She ran her fingers along the bolt just to be sure. She peered through the peephole even though she knew she wouldn't see anything in the dark.

She came back and stood behind Nicole, glancing at the front window. The blinds were perfectly still.

Nicole popped another kernel of popcorn into her mouth. "Did you see that? They almost dropped the map."

Diana didn't answer. She walked to the bedroom and re-trieved the flashlight from the drawer, then tucked it beside the couch. She sat back down, not quite as relaxed as before, the blanket still across her lap, her hand now gripping the edge.

The rest of the night passed without another sound.

But the unease didn't fade.

Later, when Nicole was asleep in her own bed and the house had gone dark, Diana lay staring at the ceiling, her ears tuned to every creak, every gust of wind. No more knocks came. No more tapping. But the memory of that growl stayed with her. It circled her thoughts like a slow, steady drumbeat.

She didn't sleep for hours.

Even when she eventually fell asleep, her rest was so light that she woke feeling no more refreshed.

CHAPTER 13

The wind stirred early that morning, sweeping across the porch in restless pulses. Diana sat with a mug of coffee cooling in her hands, listening to the trees shift and lean, their trunks creaking faintly as if whispering to one another. The air had weight to it, not from heat or storm, but from presence.

From the porch, she could just make out the distant twang of Nicole's bowstring drifting up from the trees. Another soft thump followed. Ben calmly called something out. Nicole laughed in reply. Diana smiled, just a little, imagining the two of them near the old tree stand Daniel had reinforced in the spring. Nicole was headstrong, sharp, and unshakably confident. Ben never talked down to her. He treated her like an equal, not a pre-teen. He explained without overexplaining, praised without puffing her up. Nicole soaked it in like light.

She sipped the last of her coffee and stood, stretching her arms. The field spread out before her like a golden sheet. The grass was knee-high and swayed in gentle waves that shimmered when the wind passed through. On the far side, the land dipped and sloped down into the woods where Nicole and Ben were now.

Something disrupted the rhythm.

The wind shifted again, cutting across her face with a sour, earthy sharpness that didn't belong. A putrid smell followed, like damp fur or hair steeped in rot and decay, crawling up her nose and settling in her throat until a slow nausea began to build. It wasn't new to her. She had smelled it before, on the edges of clearing trails and outside bedroom windows, a stench that meant they were close. Way too close.

At the edge of her vision, where the sunlight didn't quite reach, a shape crept through the tall grass. It wasn't a deer, and it wasn't a bear. The movement had a disturbing precision, its shoulders hunched as it crawled forward on all fours. Its arms were longer than they should have been, and the way it moved, jerky and low to the ground, reminded her of a spider or a lizard. Unease prickled her skin in waves.

As it slinked through the tall grass, a black crow dipped from the sky, cawing wildly as it swooped at the figure below. It circled once, then again, squawking in sharp bursts. It didn't stop. The bird shrieked and flapped, diving again and again above the creature's back, clearly agitated.

Massive shoulders shifted as it moved, too fluid in some ways and too rigid in others. The light hit its face just enough to catch the unmistakable reflection of its eyes. Red.

Diana's chest went cold.

She blinked once. It didn't vanish.

Red eyes. Focused in the direction of the tree line.

It was him.

Not one of the watchers she had grown used to. Not the curious ones that tossed pinecones or lingered at the clearing's edge.

This one moved with intent. Head down. Shoulders tight. Stalking.

And he was heading straight for Nicole and Ben.

She set her mug on the railing and turned sharply toward the door.

The shotgun stood in the corner by the entry, always loaded. Daniel had insisted it be kept within reach when he was away. She grabbed it, stepped outside, and ran down the porch steps with her heart pounding in her ears.

The figure was closer now. Moving through the tall grass like he had done it a thousand times, silent despite its size. The crow was still circling, flapping hard, its calls growing more frantic.

She raised the shotgun and fired into the sky.

The blast cracked like thunder, scattering a flock of birds from the trees. The crow shrieked one last time and disappeared into the canopy.

The creature stopped mid-step. For a heartbeat, he didn't move. Then he let out a sound that churned her stomach, a scream, deep and rasping, filled with rage and alarm.

He turned and vanished back the way he had come, cutting through the grass with terrifying speed, slipping into the treeline as if he had never been there.

Diana lowered the shotgun, breath shaking, ears ringing.

From the woods, two figures emerged. Nicole was sprinting ahead, eyes wide. Ben followed at a fast walk, scanning the trees with his hand near his sidearm.

"Mom!" Nicole called. "What happened?"

Diana forced calm into her voice. "Oh, I just saw a bear heading your way. I scared it off."

"Really?" Nicole glanced around, frowning.

"Yes," Diana said. "Go wash up and help me with breakfast. I'll be inside in a minute."

Nicole gave her a long look, then nodded and stepped into the house.

Ben stayed.

He came up the steps, boots brushing leaves aside, and leaned on the railing. "That wasn't a bear, was it."

Diana shook her head.

"Red eyes?"

She nodded. Her voice dropped to a whisper. "He was moving through the field. Heading straight toward where you were."

Ben looked toward the field, eyes narrowing. "It's the third time I've heard something near her in the past two weeks. Always quiet. Always close."

"I don't trust that one," Diana said. "The others always stayed near the trees. Watched. This one doesn't. He watches her. Follows her. It doesn't feel like the others."

Ben rubbed the back of his neck. "Maybe Nicole shouldn't be outside anymore. Even with one of us with her. At least not until we figure out what the hell it wants."

Diana stared at the grass where it had disappeared. The silence had returned, but it didn't feel peaceful. Not anymore.

"I've been thinking about leaving," she said. "Taking her and getting away from here."

Ben didn't speak right away. He let the thought settle in the quiet.

"Town's not far," he said finally. "You could stay with me for a while. Just until Daniel gets back."

Diana didn't answer right away. She watched the breeze roll through the grass again.

"I'd rather not scare her," she said. "She's smart. Strong. I'd like her to be aware of what's out there, but I don't want her to grow up afraid of the woods."

Ben looked toward the door. "She's not afraid. But you are."

Diana let out a breath she hadn't realized she'd been holding. "Yeah. I am."

They stood there a little longer, listening to a woodpecker in the distance.

Ben reached for the door. "Let's go in. I'll check the field later."

Diana followed, pausing once more at the edge of the porch.

The calm had returned. The stillness. But beneath it all, something watched.

And she would not let it take her daughter. Not without a fight.

CHAPTER 14

He felt a strange mix of curiosity, fascination and anger every time he saw her.

The yellow-haired one.

He had been watching her for a while now. Older. Taller. Her voice carried more weight, her movements more precise. But the eyes were the same, blue like cold sky before a storm. Wide. Searching. The same eyes as the one from the lake.

He felt a pull toward her he didn't understand.

She was not the same girl.

The one from the lake had been younger. Softer.

But they shared the same hair. The same skin. The same glance over one shoulder when startled. That was enough.

The rage inside him blurred the difference.

The girl at the lake all those years ago had screamed, and the sky machines came. The nets. The thundersticks. The blood. Everything that mattered had ended in the days that followed.

Now here was another. So much like her it made his teeth ache.

He had been watching ever since.

At first from the distant trees.

Then closer.

The clearing around her dwelling was wide, with scattered trees and the scent of smoke from hollow stones stacked together. The hairless ones inside moved through the lighted space behind the wall of clear rock. Their noises leaked into the forest at night. High-pitched bursts from the girl. Sharp-throated exchanges between the older ones. Sometimes strange rhythmic sounds thumped from inside like patterned breathing or bone tapping.

The older female often stood on the porch. Her scent was familiar. She had watched him once. Not like the others. She had not screamed. She had stared. Still. Unmoving. A challenge in her stillness.

He kept to the edge of the trees at first. Waiting. Watching.

But the yellow-haired one was always there.

She moved through the yard often. Sometimes with the larger male, sometimes with the dark-haired one who came and went. And sometimes alone.

He came closer each time.

He had learned the ways of silence. How to step without shifting twigs. How to breathe without clouding the air. How to become part of the shadows.

At night, he circled the house.

From the shadows, he watched the glows flicker behind the glass. Saw the yellow-haired one lean against the counter, her hair lit from behind. Watched her sleep through the narrow slats, curled and still.

Each time, he came closer.

The house had grown into a shape in his mind. The entrances. The strange lights that burst to life when he passed too near. The sounds of the floor creaking. The rhythm of the hairless ones within.

He had learned her scent. It drifted near the edge of the woods, sometimes carried on her clothes or skin after she had walked the paths behind the dwelling. He followed it as one follows prey, not to feed, but to understand.

But still, she did not notice.

She was not afraid.

That stirred something inside him. A bitter coil of rage and confusion. Was she mocking him? Or did she not see what he truly was?

He snarled low behind the tree line one night, watching her move inside the dwelling with the dark-haired male. They laughed, shifted around the space, and passed something between them. She ran, shrieked, and showed her teeth in the way hairless ones did when they were pleased.

The sound scraped against his skull.

He gripped a tree trunk and twisted. The bark tore under his hands. He could not unsee the nets. The way they wrapped around Veyla's limbs. The sound of her breath stopping. The thundersticks barking from above.

It had all started with a girl like her.

Now she lived without fear. Sheltered by walls and glowing stones, while his family had vanished into the sky.

He had thought about stepping forward. About letting her see. Just once. His full height. His teeth. His fury.

But something stopped him.

A memory. Not of the scream. But of the moment before. When the child by the lake had looked at him with terror.

The same terror he now wished to see again.

And yet, something held him back.

He wanted to study her. To learn how she moved, how she acted when alone. He wanted to understand why her presence pulled at his thoughts like tangled roots. But the hatred lived beside the curiosity. A hatred for all hairless ones. For what they had done. For what they had taken. The desire to harm simmered beneath the surface, rising each time he saw her step into the clearing without fear.

The conflict twisted in him. Pulling both ways. One moment he wanted to step forward and crush the walls around her. The next he only wanted to watch her sit, breathe, and exist in silence.

The yellow-haired one looked at birds the way Veyla once had. At wind in the trees. At the wild.

He hated it.

But he needed to understand it.

So he returned. Every day and night.

He lay in the tall grass. Crouched in the brush. Sat in a tree not far from the window where she slept. Sometimes he could hear her breath through the glass.

What frustrated him more was how often the older hairless ones remained near her. They did not stray far anymore. The yellow-haired one was rarely alone. The male stayed close, or the female hovered close. It made watching harder. Studying her movements required patience, and the presence of others soured the quiet he needed.

He began to pace more at night. To grunt low and angry into the soil. She belonged in the woods, yet they kept her fenced in with noise and light.

Soon, he would make them see.

CHAPTER 15

It was about three months later when the coyotes started, just after midnight. It began with distant yips, high-pitched and scattered.

Daniel stirred in the dark, eyes still closed, half-dreaming of the ocean and ice cream. Diana shifted beside him.

"Do you hear that?" she asked.

He grunted, then sat up slowly. The sound came again, louder now. Not one or two. A whole pack. Yipping, howling, barking. Layers of wild sound rising and falling, crashing into the quiet. They didn't sound far. Not at all.

Diana sat up too. The bedroom window was open slightly, and the noise poured in. It was sharp and frantic, a chaos that made it impossible to feel settled.

"They've been going for a while," Daniel said, rubbing his eyes.

"It's never like this. Not this long. Not this loud."

Daniel slipped out from under the sheet and walked barefoot to the hall. He peeked into Nicole's room. She was face-down in a tangle of blankets, breathing slow and heavy. Spent from the waterpark. A perfect day in the sun with her friends had knocked her out early.

He came back and sat on the edge of the bed. Diana was still listening, frowning.

"What do you think could set them off like this?" she asked.

"Could be anything."

"Or someone."

He looked at her.

The noise kept going. It filled every gap between the trees and seemed to pulse through the walls. Every so often, one of the coyotes would let out a howl so loud it felt like it echoed inside their chest.

They lay back down but didn't sleep. Not really.

An hour passed.

Then a scream shattered everything.

It began low, guttural, like something trying to claw its way out of its own throat. It rose and twisted into something jagged, a sound soaked in pain and fury. It didn't sound like an animal. It didn't sound human either. But it was close.

As soon as it started, the coyotes fell silent.

They stopped all at once. Like a switch had been thrown.

Diana sat up, hands over her ears. Her eyes wide, searching the dark.

"What the hell is that?" Daniel whispered.

The scream went on. Thirty seconds. Forty. Still rising. Still raw.

Nicole appeared in the doorway, eyes wide with sleep and confusion. "Mom?"

"Come here, baby."

She crossed the room and climbed in beside her mother. Diana pulled her close, one hand cradling the back of her head.

The scream cut off suddenly, as if something had snatched it from the air.

Stillness followed.

Not just quiet. There was nothing. No wind. No insects. No shift of trees. Even the house seemed to go still.

Daniel stood and crossed to the window, peeking between the blinds. Beyond them, only the black shapes of trees stood. The yard looked the same as it always did, but the feeling was different.

Nicole tucked her face into Diana's side. Diana's hand moved slowly over her daughter's back.

None of them spoke for a long time.

Eventually, sleep returned in pieces. A doze, then a jolt awake. A drifting in and out of restless silence.

****

Gray light filtered in through the kitchen the following morning. Diana moved slowly, brewing coffee while Daniel showered. Nicole had gone back to her room sometime after dawn and was still sleeping.

Daniel came into the kitchen and grabbed the shotgun from just inside the front door. He stepped outside, moving quietly. The air was still cool, the yard pale with morning light.

He stopped cold at the top of the steps.

Blood. Dark, wet, still fresh. A coyote lay sprawled in the center of the porch. Its limbs were bent at impossible angles, its mouth frozen in a snarl. The fur was streaked red. Blood had poured from its ears and nose. Its chest looked collapsed. Flattened.

Daniel scanned the yard. Nothing moved.

He stepped back inside briefly, told Diana not to let Nicole come out, then headed to the shed at the side of the house. He grabbed a shovel, still holding the shotgun in his other hand.

The porch wasn't visible from the shed, not with the house's angle blocking the view. As he rounded the corner, he muttered curses under his breath. "Freakin' mess. Every damn week it's something else," he grumbled. "Can't even get one quiet night."

He turned toward the porch.

The body was gone.

Only the blood remained, thick and gleaming on the steps.

The shovel slipped from his hand and struck the ground with a dull thud. He raised the shotgun, pivoting slowly in a circle. Eyes scanning the woods, the roofline, the treeline across the road. His breath came shorter now.

Nothing.

Not a whisper of movement. Not a sound.

He stood there for a long moment, pulse heavy in his neck.

He left the shovel where it had fallen and walked up the steps, crossing the porch in slow, careful strides. Inside, he closed the door behind him, placed the shotgun on the table, and sat down in the kitchen, unmoving.

Diana walked in and paused when she saw his face.

"What is it?"

He looked up slowly. "The body is gone."

"The coyote?"

He nodded. "I went to the shed to get the shovel. When I came back... it was just gone."

Her mouth opened, then closed again. She blinked. "Oh my god. It must have taken it. And you didn't notice or hear anything?"

Daniel shook his head. "I didn't hear a thing."

They stared at each other across the kitchen. A long minute passed.

Daniel's mind raced. He was a military man, trained to notice, to react, to sense movement, silence, threat. And yet something had come within feet of the house and taken a blood-soaked carcass without a trace. Not a sound. Not a shadow. Nothing.

Diana finally spoke. "That was a message."

Daniel didn't argue.

He just sat there, eyes fixed on the empty porch outside the window, wondering how far this thing was willing to go.

CHAPTER 16

Later that day, just after lunch, the sound of tires on the driveway carried through the living room. Daniel stood and moved to the window, pulling back the curtain. "Sheriff's here."

Diana looked up from the kitchen where she was drying dishes. "This should be good."

The cruiser eased to a stop, dust curling around the tires. Sheriff Andrew Cole stepped out like he was doing them a big favor, though town was barely eight minutes away. He adjusted his belt, spit into the dirt, and walked toward the house with that self-important stride he always had.

Daniel opened the door before the sheriff could knock. "Come in."

"Well now," Sheriff Cole said, taking off his sunglasses and tucking them into his shirt pocket. "Didn't expect to get the royal treatment."

"Thought you'd want to come inside instead of stand out in the open," Daniel replied.

The sheriff stepped inside, eyes scanning the entryway. "Still looks the same as last time I came out here. Was that... what, five years back? Nuisance bear getting into your garbage?"

"Wasn't a bear then, and it's not a bear now," Diana said, coming around the corner and wiping her hands on a dish towel.

"You sure about that?" the sheriff asked, lifting a brow. He looked around like he expected something dramatic to leap out of the furniture. "Alright then. Let's hear it."

They led him into the living room. Daniel gestured for him to take the recliner, but Sheriff Cole remained standing for a moment, surveying the place like he was already writing his report in his head. Then he sat with a groan, leaning back, hands resting on his stomach.

Diana moved toward the kitchen. "Can I get you something to drink? Water? Coffee?"

He shook his head. "Appreciate it, but I'm not staying long."

Nicole wandered in from the hallway, barefoot, her sketch-pad under one arm. She gave the sheriff a polite smile. "Hi."

He looked over at her and gave a tight nod. "You must be Nicole. Grown a bit since I last saw you."

She nodded. "I guess."

"So tell me," he said, his voice taking on that slow drawl he used when talking to people he didn't think had much to say. "You seen this Bigfoot creature your parents are worried about?"

Nicole sat on the edge of the couch. "I have seen plenty of them but not the red-eyed one. Heard him, though."

That got a little chuckle out of him. "Is that so?"

She shrugged, unfazed. "Yep. Often."

The sheriff shook his head, smiling like he was indulging a child's tall tale. "Strange. I've spent plenty of time out here and never once seen anything like that."

"Doesn't mean they haven't seen you," Nicole said, her voice calm but direct.

Daniel glanced over at her, the corners of his mouth twitching.

Sheriff Cole cleared his throat. "Any proof? Tracks? Hair? Pictures?"

Daniel answered. "No. Nothing that would convince you."

The sheriff leaned forward, elbows on his knees. "Not much I can do then."

Diana folded her arms. "We're not asking for a task force. We just want it noted. In case something happens."

He looked at her for a moment, eyes narrowing just slightly. "Something like what?"

"In case someone gets hurt," Daniel said. "Or worse."

Sheriff Cole exhaled loudly and sat back in the chair again. "Look, I'm not saying you didn't see something. Maybe it was a bear. They stand up on two legs sometimes. Maybe it was a trespasser. Maybe even some kids pulling a prank."

"No prank leaves a coyote crushed to death on your porch and then makes it vanish by the time you grab a shovel," Daniel said, glancing at Nicole before he spoke.

"And no bear screams like a siren," Diana added.

The sheriff didn't argue. He scratched his chin, then stood. "I'll let my deputies know to keep an eye out when they do their rounds at night. I'll even swing by once or twice myself."

Diana didn't look convinced. "Thanks."

He moved to the door, paused, and turned back. "But I'll say this... don't go shooting at shadows. You hit someone by mistake, that's on you."

"We're not idiots," Daniel said.

Sheriff Cole opened the door and stepped out onto the porch. The sun was lower now, casting long stretches of light across the front yard. He adjusted his hat, squinting toward the woods.

"I still say it was probably a bear."

Diana held the door as he walked out. "We wouldn't be so

concerned if it was just a bear, sheriff."

He chuffed, gave a mock salute, and walked back to his cruiser. The engine coughed to life, and he drove off without another word, the car bouncing slightly as it hit the ruts in the old driveway.

Daniel watched him go, arms crossed.

Diana closed the door and turned to him. "Well?"

Daniel shrugged. "I hate to say it, but I told ya so."

That evening, the family sat together on the couch. The TV played softly in the background, some documentary about deep sea creatures flickering across the screen. Nicole sat cross-legged, sketching again. Diana had a blanket draped over her legs. Daniel sat at the far end of the couch, remote in one hand, the other resting on his knee. His eyes were on the screen, but he wasn't really watching.

His thoughts were still back at the porch.

Still waiting in the dark.

Still thinking about red eyes.

****

In the early hours of morning, Nicole sat upright in bed, legs pulled to her chest beneath the blanket. She had heard it once already, faint and low, like a sound wrapped in dream. It had woken her, and for several minutes she lay still, unsure if she had imagined it. But now it came again, unmistakable, from the woods. Her eyes flicked to the window, where the blinds were drawn but not tightly enough to block the glow of the motion light outside.

A voice. Dragged out, like someone speaking through water.

"Niiiii-cooole…"

The syllables stretched unnaturally, as if the speaker had only ever heard the name but never said it aloud. The "N" was too sharp. The "L" floated loose at the end. The pause between the two halves of the name didn't feel human.

She didn't move.

"Niiiii… cooole…"

It came again. Wrong in tone. Too low. Too slow and intentional. Like a voice buried deep in a throat not made for words.

She slid out of bed and moved toward the door, placing her bare feet quietly on the hardwood floor.

The bedroom door creaked open from the other side.

Diana stepped into the room in her robe, face pale and tight.

"You heard it?" she whispered.

Nicole nodded.

They both turned toward the window as the motion light clicked on. Something had moved near the tree line.

Daniel was already awake. Diana had nudged him before getting up, and he now stood by the front door, boots pulled on hastily, shotgun in one hand. He didn't wait.

He opened the door and stepped onto the porch. The cold bit into his skin. He scanned the trees.

"Niiiii... cooole..."

It came again. The same stretched syllables. Less like a call, more like a trial run of language forced through the wrong mouth.

He raised the shotgun and fired into the ground toward the direction of the voice.

The blast shattered the silence.

A hoarse, dragging growl followed. It rolled across the yard like thunder, vibrating through the boards beneath his feet.

He pumped the shotgun and fired again. Another shot into the dirt. Deeper into the trees.

Silence.

Not even wind.

Daniel stood there for a long moment, shoulders tense,

watching for movement.

Nothing moved. The motion light clicked off. The darkness returned.

He backed into the house and locked the door behind him. Diana was holding Nicole by the shoulders, guiding her back to bed.

"Was that its voice?" she asked.

Daniel didn't answer.

CHAPTER 17

The sun had only just begun to rise when Ben's truck pulled into the long, cracked driveway. Mist still clung to the ground in the lower parts of the property, curling around the bases of the trees like thin smoke. Diana stood on the porch, arms folded, watching as Ben stepped out with his rifle over his shoulder.

Daniel met him at the steps, quiet but resolute. Words weren't needed. Both men understood what they planned to do.

"Let's get to it," Ben said.

Daniel ducked back inside, grabbed his shotgun from the wall just inside the front door, and reappeared. Ben already had his rifle across his shoulder. Daniel exchanged a brief look with Diana, and she told him to be safe. Nicole stood in the hallway behind her, arms crossed, eyes sharp. She didn't say anything as her father stepped off the porch.

Daniel gave her a small nod, then turned and headed into the trees with Ben.

Diana lingered in the doorway a moment longer, watching them go. Then she turned and looked at Nicole, who lingered just inside the hall.

"I have something for you," Diana said softly.

Nicole followed her into the kitchen. Diana opened a drawer, reached beneath a folded towel, and pulled out a leather-wrapped bundle. Then, she placed it gently into Nicole's hands.

"I made this for you," she said. "You're old enough now. I want you to keep it on you. Always."

Nicole unwrapped it slowly. Inside was a handcrafted knife. The blade had been forged from recycled metal, its surface polished clean, the edge sharp and slightly curved. The workmanship was exceptional, balanced, practical, built to last. The handle was carved from deer bone, pale and smoothed by hand, fitted tight to the tang. Along one side, something had been inscribed with care.

She turned the knife in her hands, nodding as she looked it over. "It's beautiful. Thanks mama!"

She stepped forward and gave Diana a hug, pressing her face briefly into her mother's shoulder. Then she wrapped the knife again and carried it back to her room without another word.

****

The forest was dense and wet from the morning dew. The silence wasn't total. Birds still stirred, and insects buzzed, but the tension in the air was real. Daniel moved in a wide arc toward the west creek, setting a loop through the 28-acre property that he and Diana had walked hundreds of times before. Today, it felt unfamiliar.

They had agreed to fire every thirty paces. Daniel would go first, then Ben. One blast from the shotgun. One crack from the rifle. Not at anything, just into the air or the ground. A warning.

The first shots echoed hard through the trees, scattering birds into the sky. Squirrels darted. Leaves shivered. But beyond that, the woods held their silence. The two men pressed on.

They moved in a wide circle, stopping every thirty paces. At first, nothing stood out. Then they began to see signs. A snapped branch here. Freshly trampled brush there. Daniel pointed out a path of flattened ferns that hadn't been there the last time he walked this side of the property.

"Not deer," he said quietly.

"No. Heavier."

They kept going.

Another shot. Then another. The birds stopped reacting. The forest quieted around them, like something else was listening.

Ben mumbled, "I don't like how still it's getting."

Daniel agreed but said nothing.

By the time they reached the far side of the property, the forest had gone completely quiet. Even the wind had eased. They paused beneath a wide pine, watching the underbrush, muscles tight, breathing low. The air felt like it was charged.

Daniel gave a signal, and they stood back to back. Slowly, they rotated, scanning every direction. Something moved.

"There," Ben hissed.

Off to their right, just beyond a knot of brambles, something darted low and fast. But before either of them could react, a rock the size of a softball whizzed past Daniel's face. He flinched, ducking sharply as it flew by, missing him by inches. Only his military reflexes had saved him. The velocity and precision of it were enough to stun him.

Without hesitation, both men fired into the direction the rock had come from. One blast after another thundered through the trees, cracking branches and tearing through brush.

Then came the scream.

High-pitched and raw, the scream tore through the stillness like something alive and wounded. It echoed off the trees and sent a jolt through both men. It wasn't human. It wasn't a coyote. But it had the weight of both. Rage and pain, tangled into something that made Daniel's skin crawl.

"Move!" he shouted.

They ran toward the sound, crashing through the brush,

firing into the ground to keep it running. The undergrowth whipped at their legs, and limbs slapped across their arms. For a moment, Daniel thought he saw it moving on all fours, low and fast, not just a blur but a shape. Broad. Covered in dark, thick hair. The creature disappeared amongst the trees, but its scream lingered in Daniel's ears.

Ben fired again, but it was already gone.

They slowed to a stop, both men panting, sweat streaking down their faces.

"I think I clipped it," Ben said, voice low.

"It didn't stop," Daniel replied, staring into the trees. "Didn't even slow down."

They stood in the silence that followed, the forest holding that unnatural hush again. Not quite fear. But something close.

"We keep walking the perimeter," Daniel said finally. "Next week. Week after that."

Ben nodded once.

They turned back toward the house, their weapons still in hand, scanning the woods as they moved. Daniel felt a flicker of something in his chest. Not victory. Not relief.

Hope.

Thin, uncertain, but present.

He just hoped it would be enough.

CHAPTER 18

Diana woke with a start, though no sound had stirred her. Her eyes opened to darkness, as if the night had sunk deep into the house and wrapped around everything. She lay still for a moment, waiting to hear some noise that might explain the jolt that pulled her from sleep. Nothing came. No creaking floorboard, no shifting wind. Just that feeling, the one she trusted more than her eyes or ears.

She sat up slowly, careful not to wake Daniel, and swung her legs over the side of the bed. Her chest felt tight. A sip of water, she told herself. Just a drink and back to bed. Nothing to worry about.

The hallway was cool and quiet. She padded barefoot past the bathroom and toward the kitchen, her hand brushing the wall as she moved. As she reached the living room, something caught her eye. A faint glow. Not from inside. From further down the hall.

Nicole's room.

Diana's steps slowed. The door was partially closed, but a soft light bled out through the crack. Not the overhead light. Something dimmer, pale and steady.

She pressed her palm lightly to the door and pushed it open just enough to peer inside.

Nicole was fast asleep, cocooned in her blankets, her cheek pressed against her pillow. The room was dark, save for the faint line of illumination seeping through the edges of the window blinds.

The motion sensor.

Diana's breath caught. She moved across the room on instinct, step by slow step, until she reached the window. She paused beside it, her hand hovering near the blind cord. The light wasn't flickering. It stayed on, as if something remained out there. Something large enough to keep the sensor triggered.

She touched the edge of the blind and eased it downward just enough to peek out.

The eyes were already looking at her.

She gasped and stumbled backward, her hand flying to her chest. Her knees buckled, and she caught herself on Nicole's desk.

Red Eyes.

He was crouched low, shoulders hunched, his head tilted to one side as he looked straight into Nicole's window. He was massive, his bulk blocking out the rest of the window. The eyes, those awful red eyes, were shining with terrifying clarity.

His skin looked like dark stone, slick and cracked, like charcoal soaked in oil. His hair was a mess of knots and tangles, matted and wild. And his mouth.

She felt the air leave her lungs.

His upper lip was curled back in a snarl. Not quite a smile. Something meaner. More personal. Like he knew she was watching. Like he wanted her to see.

Diana stumbled toward the door, her eyes still locked on the window. Nicole hadn't stirred. The girl breathed deeply, unbothered by the horror standing just feet away.

She stood in the doorway, her back to the wall, trying to steady her breathing. Her heart thudded in her throat. Every instinct told her to wake Nicole, to grab her and run, but she didn't. Not yet.

She waited. And he just stayed there.

After what felt like a lifetime, the motion sensor light blinked off. She dared a glance toward the window.

Darkness.

She didn't know if he had moved or if the sensor had simply timed out. But she couldn't stay. She backed into the hallway and moved straight into the bathroom.

She gripped the edge of the sink and dry heaved once, then vomited hard. The shock of it made her knees shake. She rinsed her mouth, wiped her face, and stood over the basin for a long time. Finally, she splashed cold water on her cheeks, breathing in through her nose, out through her mouth. Slow and steady.

She made her way to the bedroom, each step cautious.

Daniel shifted as she entered. He rolled toward her as she sat down on the edge of the bed.

"What's wrong?" he mumbled.

She didn't look at him right away. Just sat, her eyes fixed on the floor.

"We need to send Nicole away."

Daniel blinked. "What? Why?"

She turned to him slowly. Her face was ashen.

"He was just at her window. Red Eyes."

Daniel sat up, fully awake now.

"Are you sure?"

She nodded. "I saw him. He was hunched down. Watching her. Inches away. His face... he was snarling. Like he knew I'd see him."

Daniel started to swing his legs over the side of the bed.

"Leave it," she said quietly. "He's already gone."

He froze, met her eyes, then leaned back on his elbows.

A few minutes later, Diana returned to Nicole's room and

sat beside her daughter. The girl had stirred but hadn't woken fully. Diana ran a hand over her hair, whispering softly. Her body still shook.

****

Late morning, Diana stepped outside to bring in the laundry. Daniel followed her, the shotgun cradled in one arm. He stayed on the back deck, eyes sweeping the yard, grinding his teeth. The air had a heaviness to it after the night they'd had.

Diana reached the line and stopped. Her hand hovered over a clothespin, but her eyes were on the space where Nicole's Pat Benatar t-shirt should have been.

"Nicole's T-shirt is gone," she said.

Daniel took a step off the deck, gaze narrowing. "You sure it didn't just blow off?"

"I can't see it anywhere," she said, scanning the yard, the surrounding grass, the low shrubs near the tree line. The rest of the laundry hung undisturbed, barely swaying in the light breeze. Just that one shirt was missing.

Daniel moved slowly through the grass, checking the length of the yard with careful eyes. He circled the shed, peered under the back steps, and even stepped out toward the long grass at the edge of the clearing. The shirt was nowhere to be found.

He didn't say anything. Just turned and looked at the woods.

Diana watched him from the clothesline.

He nodded once and stepped into the grass, still carrying the shotgun. His pace was slow, eyes scanning the brush ahead of him. As soon as he crossed into the shadow of the trees, a foul stench hit him. His nose curled. Sweat, rot and something worse. Something old.

He paused and listened.

The woods were quiet.

About six yards into tree line, he found the shirt. Draped over a snapped branch like it had been purposely placed there.

His stomach turned.

He stepped closer, and locked eyes on something he didn't expect to see.

Beneath the branch, half-hidden by ferns and leaves, lay a crude bed of sticks and grass. It had been shaped with intention. Flattened. Sunken. Used. The surrounding ground was disturbed, the underbrush trampled down.

And it reeked.

Daniel stepped back gradually, turning to scan the area. He followed a thin break in the trees, a narrow tunnel through the undergrowth.

And saw the house.

Nicole's bedroom window.

Visible. Clear.

He stood there, the weight of it all crashing in at once. The shirt. The bed of sticks. The line of sight.

He shifted his grip on the shotgun.

He could feel the heat of rage and fear rising, but he controlled his breathing, steadying each inhale to keep a level head.

This needed to end.

CHAPTER 19

Ben's truck crunched along the gravel as he pulled into the Beretti driveway just after breakfast. The sky was overcast, and the breeze carried a faint chill. He stepped out, glanced around the property and made his way to the front door.

Diana opened it before he could knock. Her face looked tired, but she smiled when she saw him.

"Hey," she said.

"Hey yourself."

From down the hallway, Nicole's door creaked open. She came into the living room, still in pajamas, her hair a tangle.

"Uncle Ben?"

He turned to her with a smile. "You up for a little trip? Thought we'd go see the ocean. Got a break in my schedule, figured we should take advantage."

Nicole's eyes lit up. "Really?"

He nodded. "Just a few days. Thought we could hit the coast, get some fresh air, maybe eat too much ice cream. What do you say?"

She looked to her mother, eyebrows raised in hopeful excitement.

Diana smiled. "Yes. You can go."

"Yes!" Nicole darted down the hall toward her room. "I'm gonna pack my backpack."

Ben stepped inside and closed the door. He set the overnight bag down gently.

Diana approached him quietly. Her voice dropped to a low murmur. "Thank you. We really appreciate it."

Ben glanced toward the hallway where Nicole had vanished, then back to Diana. "Of course. Daniel talked to me this morning. I'm more than happy to do it. Just... what's he planning while we're gone?"

Diana exhaled, her arms folding. "I don't know. But we have to do something. That thing, Red Eyes, it's getting bolder. It was right at her window. It's only a matter of time before it tries something."

Ben nodded, his expression grave. "I'll keep her safe. You know that."

Daniel came down the hall then, tugging his flannel sleeves into place.

"Hey, brother. Thanks again."

"Anytime," Ben said. He clapped him on the shoulder. "You

two just be careful, alright?"

Nicole emerged from her room with a bright blue backpack, half-zipped and bulging with clothes and books.

"I'm ready!"

"That was fast," Daniel said with a small smile.

"I didn't want to forget anything. I even brought snacks."

Ben grinned. "Good. Always important."

Nicole hugged her dad tight, then moved to Diana. Diana held her a little longer than usual.

"I love you, sugar booger."

"Love you too, Mom."

Daniel bent down, kissed the top of her head. "Love you, kiddo. Be good."

Nicole beamed. "Love you, Dad."

They walked out to the truck. Ben opened the passenger side for her, and Nicole climbed in, already chatting about what kind of ice cream she wanted first.

Diana and Daniel stood at the door, watching as the truck rolled down the driveway.

Just before it turned onto the road, both of them called out, "You be good!"

Nicole leaned out the window and waved back. "I'll be better than good. I'll be great!"

The truck disappeared around the bend.

Diana closed the door slowly.

Daniel stood for a moment, staring at the empty driveway.

"She'll be alright," Diana said quietly.

He nodded, though his jaw clenched.

"It's time we figure out how to end this."

CHAPTER 20

Diana had spent the day baking. She told herself it was to stay productive, to prepare something for her neighbor, Dora Richards, like she had promised. But the truth clung closer. She needed to keep her mind occupied. She needed her hands to stay moving, her thoughts buried in crusts and fillings, flour, and spice, not drifting toward the woods. Not wandering toward that face in the window. That stare.

The kitchen was warm and sweet-smelling, full of cinnamon and cooked apples. Her apron was dusted in flour, and the tips of her fingers were pale from overhandling dough. Outside, the sun was beginning to slip behind the trees, dimming the yard with a soft, creeping dusk.

Daniel was in the driveway with the hood of the truck up, working with his sleeves rolled up. He'd told her earlier that he needed time to think, that working on the truck helped clear his head. It was where he came up with his best ideas. His shotgun was propped against the truck within easy reach. Every now and then she could hear the clang of tools or the low grumble of a wrench refusing to turn. That noise helped too. It meant he was close.

Nicole was gone for a few days with Ben. Safe. The word echoed in her head every hour. Safe.

The pie sat cooling on the counter, golden and still faintly steaming. She had already wrapped it in a cloth-lined basket but hadn't found the energy to walk it down the road. Dora had insisted Edwin would swing by to grab it, and that suited her just fine. She didn't want to leave the house.

A short while later, she stepped out onto the porch with the basket in her hands. Daniel was half under the truck, tools scattered in a tidy arc near the tarp. She leaned against one of the porch posts and watched him work.

Then Edwin Richards appeared at the bend in the drive.

He walked slowly, wearing a cap pulled low and a light jacket. His gait was careful, slow but steady. She smiled and lifted a hand in greeting.

He raised his hand in return. "Evening."

"Evening, Edwin," she replied, her voice calm despite the twist in her gut. The light was changing fast. She hated that time of day. It made the trees darker. Hiding places, not just woods.

Daniel slid out from beneath the truck, standing and wiping his hands on a rag. He smiled faintly and nodded at Edwin. "Right on time."

Edwin laughed. "I came to collect before it vanished. Heard

cinnamon was involved."

Diana handed him the basket. "Still warm."

Edwin's expression softened. "Dora'll be over the moon. Thank you."

They stood there for a moment, chatting about nothing much. Daniel asked about the weather report, Edwin mentioned some story from the co-op. Diana half-listened. Her fingers rubbed idly at the flour still clinging to her skin.

Edwin tilted his head. "Where's Peanut?"

Diana answered, "Ben took her on a road trip for a few days. Gave us some space to figure out what to do about our sasquatch problem."

A heavy flapping sound hit the roof above her.

She looked up. A crow had landed near the chimney, large and ragged-looking. It squawked, loud and frantic, its head bobbing as it stared down at her.

Her heart dropped.

She glanced at Daniel and saw him turn his head.

He froze.

Diana saw the way his shoulders locked, how the color drained from his face. A cold feeling crept up her spine as she followed his gaze.

Red Eyes stood at the edge of the clearing.

The creature's hulking form stood out against the dark timberline, blacker than the trees, as if he absorbed what little light remained. His eyes burned red. His posture was low and rigid, like a predator waiting for the signal to spring.

Daniel took a step back and grabbed the shotgun beside the truck.

"Stay still," he said, his voice low.

Edwin didn't argue. He just stared, terrified.

Red Eyes launched from the tree line on all fours, moving with a horrible, fluid grace. His fingers splayed as he ran, claws tearing through grass and soil. His growl began low, then grew, like something ancient rising from the pit of the earth.

Diana screamed.

Daniel raised the shotgun and fired. The flash lit up Red Eyes mid-stride, but he didn't slow. He charged straight through the shot like he didn't feel it.

"Get in the car," Daniel yelled.

They ran towards Diana's car. Edwin dove into the back seat while Diana scrambled into the front passenger side. Daniel jumped into the driver's seat and threw the car into gear.

Gravel exploded beneath the tires. Dust spiraled in their wake. The rear end of the car fishtailed before catching the road. Daniel gripped the wheel tight, foot pressed hard to the floor.

Diana twisted around in her seat, eyes scanning the trees. "I can't see him," she said, frantic, turning again to check behind them.

Daniel's eyes darted between the road and his mirrors. His hands were white on the wheel. Sweat beaded on his forehead, his breath coming hard and fast.

In the back seat, Edwin braced his arms on either side, palms planted into the vinyl. He mumbled prayers under his breath, his eyes squeezed shut.

A flash of black darted from the treeline to Diana's right, huge and fast, and she caught a glimpse through the side window.

Red Eyes.

His arms were pumping. His mouth was open. His eyes locked with hers.

She screamed.

A heartbeat later, Red Eyes slammed into the car. The impact struck the side like a wrecking ball, sending the vehicle spinning off the road and into a ditch. The world tilted violently. Tires lost contact. The car rolled once, then slammed back down on its wheels with a jolt that rattled every bone in their bodies.

Diana's shoulder hit the door hard. Edwin let out a sharp grunt as he slammed sideways into the back seat. Daniel's forehead struck the steering wheel, and blood ran down his face in a dark, steady line.

He gasped, dazed, eyes flicking downward.

The shotgun had fallen during the crash, wedged between the seat and the door. He reached for it, fingers straining.

The windshield was already cracked from the roll.

A massive fist punched through the damaged glass, shards flying.

Daniel's hand was inches from the weapon when Red Eyes grabbed him by the neck and pulled him out through the windshield in a second like he weighed nothing.

Diana screamed. She desperately searched for the shotgun. Her fingers closed around the stock and she yanked it free, trying to rack it, but the mechanism jammed. Her hands were slick with sweat and blood. She fumbled, terrified.

Outside, Red Eyes let out a horrible sound and dragged Daniel into the trees. His limbs bounced across the dirt, then disappeared.

The screams stopped quickly.

Diana pushed at the door with her good arm, but it was stuck. She tried kicking it open, panic rising in her throat.

Red Eyes returned. He reached back through the opening.

Diana kicked and fought, but he caught her by the head

and shoulder. With an effortless pull, he hauled her through the broken glass. The force dislocated her shoulder as she was yanked from the car.

She caught one last glimpse of Edwin's face in the back seat.

His expression was frozen in horror.

Then she hit the ground hard. Red Eyes grabbed her head and flung her toward the nearest tree. Her body struck the trunk and collapsed in a heap.

Her final thought was of Nicole.

Red Eyes returned to the car. He lunged through the shattered windshield, trying to reach Edwin. But the roof had collapsed enough to block his grasp. His claws scraped along twisted metal, his breath heaving, hot and sour.

He snarled, frustrated. Beat his fists against the crumpled hood.

Then he backed away.

Edwin lay motionless, pinned and soon passed out.

Red Eyes let out a grunt. Almost a huff.

And walked back into the woods.

Leaving the car. Leaving the blood. Leaving Nicole an orphan.

CHAPTER 21

-PRESENT DAY-

The clang of weights echoed through the gym, the scent of rubber flooring, metal and sweat hanging in the air. Nicole Beretti finished her final set of pull-ups, jaw set, breath controlled. She dropped to the floor and shook out her arms, flexing her fingers to work out the heat.

Noah Jacobi was on the bench press behind her, grunting through a final rep. He racked the bar with a loud clank and sat up, catching his breath.

"You trying to prove something again?" he asked, wiping his forehead with a towel.

Beretti gave him a sidelong look and grabbed her towel. "Just staying sharp."

"You're something else. You train like you're prepping for the apocalypse."

"Always gotta be prepared."

Jacobi stood and stretched, rotating his back with a few

pops. "Well, it definitely looks like you are."

Beretti gave a slight smile and picked up her water bottle. "Thanks."

They finished up and wiped down their equipment. The gym was small and functional, nothing flashy, just worn machines, a heavy bag that sagged in the middle, and lighting that buzzed softly above. A few locals worked out in silence, heads down, giving Beretti and Jacobi an occasional glance.

As they stepped outside, the cold met them with a quiet bite. It was late morning, the air dry and still. Blackridge didn't get snow, but winter still made itself known. They walked toward Main Street, passing stores and cafes. A breeze moved down the street, tugging at jackets and raising collars.

Jacobi noticed it first. The looks.

Men at the hardware store, the teenager stacking boxes outside the grocer, the guy loading lumber into his truck, each one subtly turned their head as Beretti passed. Some tried not to stare. The rest didn't even try.

He leaned closer. "You know people can't help looking at you, right?"

She didn't even glance at him. "They're curious. Outsiders in a small town draw attention."

"Curious is one word for it."

Their usual spot, an old-school diner with fogged windows

and the smell of bacon that never quite left, was open and half full. The waitress gave them a nod of recognition as they stepped in. They slid into the booth in the corner, the one that gave them a view of the whole room and both exits.

Jacobi rubbed his hands together. "This place always smells like breakfast and floor polish. In a good way."

Beretti picked up the menu, even though she already knew what she'd order. "You said you had a friend up north?"

"Yeah. Oregon. Eugene, technically. I'm gonna go see him in a few weeks."

She raised a brow. "Haven't heard you talk about anyone from back in the day."

Jacobi gave a small shrug. "Yeah, Nate is a college roommate. We stay in touch via text or email. He's a lawyer now, of all things. Climbs rocks for fun, writes legal briefs during the week. Weird combination, but it suits him."

"Does he know what you do in the Bureau?"

Jacobi smiled, a bit sheepishly. "Some of it. Not the cryptid stuff. You start talking about creatures and disappearances and secret reports, and people either stop calling or start thinking you're full of it. Or they figure out what's really going on and start asking questions we're not allowed to answer."

Beretti nodded. "Too many questions and they figure out the government already knows and keeps it quiet."

"Exactly. So I keep it simple. Tell him I'm in investigations, federal cases, that sort of thing."

She took a sip of coffee the waitress had just placed in front of her. It was hot and strong, the way she liked it. She stared out the window for a moment, watching a truck roll by with a load of hay in the back.

Jacobi tilted his head. "You okay?"

She nodded slowly. "Just thinking."

"About your parents?"

"Yeah."

He let the silence sit briefly, then reached for his own mug. "We'll get him."

Beretti's voice was calm but certain. "I know."

They were nearly finished with lunch when Beretti's phone buzzed. She glanced at the screen and answered. It was Deputy Ellis. He asked if she and Jacobi could check in with a local man, an old friend of his, who claimed to have seen a Sasquatch.

Beretti said they would handle it. "Text me the address," she told him. "We'll head out now."

As she ended the call, she hoped it was a sighting of Red Eyes.

CHAPTER 22

They reached the property in the early afternoon. It sat about five miles north of Blackridge, tucked back from the road. A light wind stirred the tall grass along the gravel drive, carrying the faint, earthy scent of sun-warmed pasture. A narrow track led up to a modest two-story cabin with a front porch. The place was well kept and clearly maintained, blending neatly into its natural surroundings.

Beretti parked the SUV near a patch of packed earth beside the porch. A man stepped out of the doorway as they approached. Early thirties, lean, with a sun-creased face and sharp eyes. He wore a faded hoodie, worn jeans, and scuffed work boots. His cap was low over his forehead, and his hands were shoved into his pockets.

"Y'all the agents?" he asked.

Beretti nodded. "Special Agent Beretti. This is Special Agent Jacobi."

He gave them both a small nod. "I'm Craig. Uh... Craig Dalton. Come on in."

Inside, the cabin smelled of burnt coffee, old wood and the

faint tang of gun oil. A few pictures hung on the walls, family shots, hunting trophies, and a framed American flag. A pair of boots sat near the door, mud still crusted to the soles. He led them to the small kitchen table. The floor creaked as they moved.

They all sat down. Craig rubbed his palms along the tops of his thighs, then tapped his fingers against the edge of the table.

"I... uh, appreciate y'all comin' out here. I wasn't sure if this was the kinda thing the FBI even... dealt with. But Ellis said to talk to you. Said you'd listen."

Beretti nodded. "He said you saw something. Something strange."

"Yeah," Craig said, looking down. "Yeah. Somethin' real strange."

He was quiet for a second, rubbing his jaw, eyes flicking toward the window like he was making sure the woods hadn't crept closer.

He exhaled. "Okay. So... look. Ten nights ago. Maybe eleven now. My brother, Damian, he calls me up around two in the mornin'. He'd been drinkin' at this place up in Lancaster. Just a bar, kinda run-down, but they stay open late. His missus, she, uh, refused to get up and drive him. Said she wasn't leavin' her warm bed for that drunk idiot, her words."

He gave a nervous chuckle, then rubbed a hand over his face.

"So... I head out. I'd just bought this new Ram, like, real new. Had that dealership smell still. Pick him up, he's drunk but not belligerent, just runnin' his mouth like usual. Talkin' about football, politics, Mama. She just went into a home a few weeks back, so it's been kinda heavy. Anyway... I drive him out to his place. He lives three miles past mine, on Enterprise Road."

Craig leaned forward a bit, elbows on the table.

"I pull into the driveway and we just... sit there. Still cold out. Windows startin' to fog. We're just talkin'. Kinda quiet. He says to me, real sudden-like, 'Did you hear that?' I say, 'Hear what?' He says, 'Like a growl.' I didn't hear nothin' at first. Figured his belly was grumblin'."

He swallowed and shook his head.

"But then... I heard it. It was so low. Not like a dog or a coyote. This was... deeper. Like it was comin' up through the ground."

Jacobi's expression darkened slightly. He said nothing.

"I turned around in my seat, tryin' to look out the back window, but it was fogged. So I put my foot on the brake to light it up a little. And... man, I swear, there was somethin' back there. Freakin' big. Just a silhouette, but it wasn't no tree. Wasn't no bear. It looked like a person, only... bigger. Way bigger."

Beretti leaned in slightly. "What happened next?"

Craig blinked a few times. His fingers fidgeted with the

edge of the table.

"We heard footsteps," he said, almost whispering. "Big ones. On two feet. Walkin' real slow. Around to the driver's side, my side. I froze up. I didn't even look. Just... stared straight ahead. I had a feelin' that I didn't wanna see whatever it was. My brother was mumblin' stuff, like prayin', but nothin' that made sense. And we both felt it. This... this weight. Ya know the dread that hits you before somethin' awful happens. It felt like we were done. I couldn't explain it."

His voice trembled.

"Then this... thing... leaned down and looked in through the windshield. Right in my face. I about pissed myself. I ain't ashamed to say it. It was... awful. Just ugly. Skin like... I don't know, like cracked leather or somethin'. Hair was long and matted, like it'd been dragged through a swamp. But the eyes... they were the freakiest eyes I'd ever seen..."

He trailed off, shaking his head again.

"They were red. Not like from a flashlight or a reflection. Just... red. Like blood red. It looked at me, then at my brother, without even movin' its head. Just shifted those damn eyes over. And then it bared its teeth. The thing's teeth were yellow and huge. It had canines like we do, but the rest were more like a horse's. I don't know why I remember this, but its gums were black, and the skin around its teeth was this bright pink. The look on its face... it wasn't tryin' to scare us. It looked furious. Like it freakin' hated us."

He took a deep breath. "Sorry, guys," he said, voice low. "This thing just freaked the shit outta me."

Beretti nodded gently. "It's okay. Take your time."

He adjusted in his seat before continuing.

"Okay. So, I snapped outta it and threw the truck into reverse. That's when it slammed its hand, fist, whatever, down on the hood. Dented it deep. I floored it and Damian's yellin' 'Go, go!' like I needed any more encouragement."

Craig rubbed his hands together.

"We made it maybe two miles before the truck sputtered out and died. Couldn't get it goin' again. I think that thing must've busted somethin' when it slammed its hand down on the hood. No phone service, of course. And neither of us was about to step outside. We stayed in that cab till the sun came up. Talked about makin' a run for my place, but every time we thought about it, we'd just... freeze. Thing is, if that thing wanted in the truck, it coulda got in easy. It was massive, built like the Hulk. But still... sittin' in there felt better than walkin' out in the open."

Beretti finally spoke. "You guys went through a lot. You did the right thing calling us."

Craig nodded once, his hands slightly shaking.

"My brother... he won't talk about it. Refuses. Like it never happened. Me? I can't stop thinkin' about it. What it was. Why it was there. Why it didn't just... kill us. It coulda. We'd be long gone by now, no one would ever know."

Beretti asked gently, "Do you have any firearms at home?"

Craig pointed to his hip. "Had this on me that night. .38. But honestly? Might as well've been a paperweight. That thing was... huge. Nine foot easy. Built like a tank. Gun wouldn't have done a damn thing but piss it off."

Jacobi pulled a card from his pocket and slid it across the table. "If Damian ever decides he's ready to talk, even just a little, give us a call."

Craig nodded and picked up the card. "He probably won't. But I'll keep it just in case."

Beretti stood and looked toward the window. "Do you mind giving us his address? We'd just like to check the area out."

"Sure. I'll write it down."

He scribbled the address on the back of an envelope and handed it over. They walked toward the door. Craig followed.

Before they stepped out, he stopped them.

"Never believed the stories before," Craig said, shaking his head. "Always figured it was just campfire talk or pranks ya know. I still can't believe I saw a freakin' Bigfoot and I wish to God I hadn't."

He glanced toward the tree line, quiet for a moment.

Beretti followed his gaze. "It gets easier," she said.

Craig turned back to her. "So... you've seen 'em before?"

"More times than we can count," she replied. "Once you know they're real, it changes how you see the world. Everything shifts a little."

Craig gave a slow nod. "Yeah. Feels like that already."

"If you ever feel like talkin' about it again," she added, "try to find people who've had their own sightings. Folks who haven't seen one usually don't get it. And like I said, you can always give us a call."

"Yeah. Okay. Thanks," Craig said, rubbing the back of his neck. "I'll keep that in mind."

They stepped back out into the cooling evening.

Jacobi glanced toward the treeline. "Sounds like Red Eyes is still active."

Beretti didn't answer. Just stared down the drive.

CHAPTER 23

The quiet whirr of Ben's printer filled the study as Beretti leaned over the desk, eyes scanning the screen. The soft light from the desk lamp caught the tension in her jaw, though she didn't seem to notice. She'd been combing through data for hours, only pausing to jot notes or double-check a name.

Jacobi appeared in the doorway, still holding a mug of coffee that had been reheated at least twice. "You called?"

She pointed at the screen without looking up. "Yeah. Come check this out."

He crossed the room and leaned behind her, one hand braced on the back of her chair. "What am I looking at?"

"These are all the reports of Sasquatch sightings or encounters within three counties of Blackridge," she said, tapping with her pen. "Over a thirty-year span."

His eyebrows lifted. "That many?"

"More than I expected."

Jacobi whistled low under his breath. "Damn. What is this? State records?"

"No," she said. "I'm logged into the National Cryptid Database."

He pulled back slightly. "That's a real thing?"

"It is," she said, smirking. "Though not public. Or widely known."

Jacobi gave her a sideways glance. "And you got access... how?"

She shot him a flat look. "A lot of arm twisting. Ward gave me a temporary passcode. Told me not to let it expire without downloading what I needed."

He nodded slowly. "I'm impressed."

Beretti tilted her head and gave him a mock squint. "You saying I'm not normally persuasive?"

"I'm saying Ward must like you more than he likes me."

"Ward doesn't like anyone. I just caught him in a good mood."

Jacobi sipped his coffee and squinted at the screen again. "So what are you doing with it?"

"Correlating it with the data we already have. I'm narrowing the field to only the sightings that mention red eyes specifically. If this thing has a pattern, I want to find it."

He nodded and stepped aside as she clicked through the tabs, her fingers moving quickly over the keyboard. She copied coordinates, dates and names into her working document. Some of the reports were one-liners filed by local law enforcement, others were three-page incident accounts from frightened campers, homeowners or shaken hunters.

Thirty minutes passed. Jacobi stayed quiet, only breaking the silence once to refill their mugs. Outside, the wind pushed against the windows, rattling the branches of Ben's old fig tree against the glass.

Beretti finally sat back, cracked her neck, and hit "Print."

"You done?"

"For now," she said. "I filtered out every report that didn't mention red eyes. Then I ran a basic color-coding filter."

Beretti clicked through a few final steps, then opened the print queue. "Green dots are reports older than fifteen years. Yellow are between six and fifteen. Orange is from the last five years. Blue? Those are all within the last twelve months."

The printer came to life, spitting out a few freshly marked pages. She pulled the top sheet off and spread it across the table. Dozens of colored dots peppered the region, but the pattern was unmistakable.

Jacobi frowned and dragged his finger along the edge of the marked zone. "Seems like this is his territory and he doesn't stray too far away from it. Something's keeping him here."

Beretti nodded again, quieter this time. "Seems like it."

Jacobi leaned on the table and let out a breath. "Playing devil's advocate here. How sure are you that these aren't just people jumping on the cryptid bandwagon? You know how it goes. One report hits the local news, and suddenly everyone sees something in the dark."

"I ran that filter too," she said. "Cross-referenced with law enforcement records, hospital reports, wildlife calls, even roadkill data. These sightings weren't media driven. Most of them were never reported publicly."

She tapped one of the blue dots again.

"This one came from a farmer who found a mangled goat in his field. Two miles west of the Dalton incident. Another was a woman who said something slapped the back of her trailer at two in the morning. She never reported it, just posted on a closed online forum. Her property borders the forest."

Jacobi looked over the printouts again, scanning the colored dots. "Some of these go back over twenty years."

Beretti nodded. "Yeah. It fits with the encounters on my parents' property."

Jacobi rubbed his chin. "So what's our move?"

"First, I want to get boots on the ground in that five-mile zone. Not to hunt. To observe. Track. We need to know if Red Eyes is still in the area."

Jacobi looked out the window, thoughtful. "And if he is?"

"Then we'll take him down."

Jacobi didn't say anything for a long moment. Then, gently, "You sure you're okay doing this?"

Beretti didn't answer right away. Her hand rested flat against the paper, right over the tight circle of red ink.

"I've been chasing monsters for years, Jacobi. I think it's time I finally face one."

He nodded once.

"Alright," he said. "Let's find him."

Beretti gave a faint smile. "Tomorrow morning, we go walking."

They stood together in the dim light of the study, the printer quiet now, the room filled with the low tick of Ben's old wall clock.

And somewhere in those woods, Red Eyes was stalking the dark.

CHAPTER 24

Victor and Mallory had left Reno earlier that day, the windows down and spirits high. They were on the first leg of their road trip to British Columbia, taking the scenic route. Tonight, they planned to stop near Lake Shasta, maybe grab a decent meal and crash at one of the lodges along the highway. It was their first trip in years, something they both had looked forward to.

Victor tapped the steering wheel and sang along quietly to the radio. The sun was still up, but leaning westward. 3.55 p.m. by the dashboard clock.

Mallory scrolled through the photos on her phone, barely focused on any of them. Every so often, she glanced up at the passing scenery outside the window, then went right back to scrolling.

Victor hit the brakes hard.

"Whoa!" Mallory snapped, grabbing the handle above the window. "What are you doing, babe?"

"Shit. Sorry. Did you see that?" he asked, eyes flicking to the right side of the road.

"What?" she asked, annoyed.

He threw the car into reverse, the shoulder gravel grinding beneath the tires as he backed up twenty yards.

"There. Just there. Someone ran through the woods. Dressed in all black. I swear to God, it looked like someone from the NBA. The guy was huge."

Mallory sat up straighter, squinting toward the forest line. Trees stood spaced out, their bare winter limbs giving an unusually clear view deep into the woods.

Victor pointed. "See that black stump over there? Right there."

"Yeah," she said. "It's a stump. A tree stump."

Victor shook his head. "I think that's a Bigfoot. I saw something run through there, and now all I see is that stump. Whatever I saw turned into that."

Mallory rolled her eyes. "Seriously babe? It is just a stump in the woods."

Victor reached into the back seat and grabbed his DSLR.

He popped the door open and stepped out.

"Where are you going?" Mallory asked.

"Just gonna check it out. Wait here, I won't be long."

Mallory shook her head and waved him off. As he crossed

the road, she called after him, "Don't be long, I'm starving."

He nodded and kept walking, then turned back to her with a scrunched-up nose. "Ugh. Something must've died out here. Smells like rot."

"Eww," Mallory said and pushed her window up.

Victor walked slowly across the two-lane highway and onto the shoulder.

As he stepped off the gravel, a crow flapped down onto a low-hanging branch nearby and let out a sharp, grating squawk.

Victor barely glanced at it. "Yeah, yeah," he mumbled. The bird took off, wings beating hard as it vanished into the trees.

The forest beyond the ditch was open enough to navigate without trouble. He stayed low, trying not to draw attention. The air had a heavy, still quality. No insects. No forest sounds. Nothing.

His instincts started buzzing deep in his chest. Run. Get the hell out of here. But his curiosity pulled him forward like a string wound tight.

He raised the camera and took a shot. Then another. The black stump, or what he still told himself might be a stump, was about seventy yards away. He kept snapping pictures, adjusting his angle. It felt too quiet.

Back in the car, Mallory glanced at her phone again. No

signal. She sighed and tossed it into her lap. Looking out the windshield, she saw Victor crouch slightly, still fiddling with his camera.

Victor inched closer. Forty yards. Thirty. Twenty. His breathing slowed, not from calm, but from focus.

The stump stood there. Still.

Maybe it's just a stump.

Victor glanced back at the car and took a few more steps, lowering his camera.

The stump stood up.

It rose slowly, unnaturally. Like something mechanical, jerky and yet fluid all at once. The shape became clear. At least nine feet tall. Broad as a barn door. Its hair was dark, matted, and full of grime and twigs. Its eyes were wide. Glowing red, not like a reflection, but lit from within. Its head seemed set into its traps, like it had no neck, just thick cords of muscle from its skull to its massive shoulders.

The creature's shoulders rose and fell as it stared directly at Victor, lips curled back to reveal large, yellow teeth, its eyes wide with something that looked like pleasure twisted into rage.

A wave of nausea surged through Victor. His mind screamed at him to run, but his feet refused to move. He couldn't process what he was seeing. His brain simply refused to accept it.

Then it began making a deep ooomph, ooomph, ooomph sound.

Back in the car, Mallory's mouth opened.

"Victor," she whispered. It was all she could say.

Victor felt something warm run-down his leg. He'd pissed himself.

The creature moved. In a heartbeat it crossed the distance, its limbs pumping like pistons. Victor barely flinched.

It was on him. The first swipe nearly knocked him off his feet. The second came down hard, hitting like a wrecking ball. His body folded. He didn't even have time to register the pain.

The camera slipped from his hands and hit the ground with a dull thud.

The creature gripped his head and yanked.

It came off in one clean rip.

The head landed somewhere in the brush, forgotten.

The Sasquatch glanced down at the camera, then stomped on it, crushing it underfoot. It stood there for a breath, then picked up the body like it weighed nothing and vanished into the forest.

Mallory's breath caught. Her eyes stayed locked on the clearing. Her limbs refused to move.

A single sob escaped.

Then another.

She slid slowly down into the floorboard of the front passenger seat. Curled into herself, shaking uncontrollably.

And sobbed.

CHAPTER 25

The cruiser's clock read 4:31 p.m. Deputy Jeremy Apps was still chatting with his wife, Melissa, through the Bluetooth system, their voices low and easy as they talked about dinner and the kids' homework.

"You want me to pick up something on the way home?" he asked, glancing in the rearview.

"Only if it's something green," she said with a laugh. "No more chili dogs this week."

He smiled. "Fine. I'll grab some of those pre-made salads you like. Make a man suffer."

She chuckled. "Thanks, babe. Drive safe."

"Always do."

As he rounded a bend just outside Lancaster, his headlights washed over a red sedan sitting quietly along the shoulder of Highway 5. No lights. No movement. Parked too neatly to be abandoned but too still for comfort. The windows looked fogged, and the fading light made the scene feel off.

Jeremy squinted and slowed the cruiser, flipping on the

hazards before easing off the road and coming to a stop ten feet behind it.

He took a moment before getting out, tapping the steering wheel thoughtfully. The wind tugged at the edges of his jacket as he stepped into the cold, grabbed his flashlight from the holster beside the seat, and shut the door behind him.

As he walked toward the vehicle, the wind picked up, rustling the dried roadside grass and making the trees creak gently in the distance. His boots made soft sounds against the gravel shoulder, and his breath fogged in the air.

He approached the driver's side and shone the flashlight through the window.

Empty.

He swept the beam over to the passenger side. A shape sat slumped in the seat. He leaned in closer. A woman, head covered by her arms, unmoving.

"Ma'am?" he called out.

Nothing.

He raised his voice a little. "Ma'am, are you alright?"

Still no response.

Jeremy moved around the front of the car and tapped twice on the passenger window. "Ma'am?"

Her head twitched, then lifted slowly. Her face was blotchy

and puffy, her eyes red and swollen from crying. She looked dazed, like she didn't quite understand what she was seeing.

He angled the flashlight away. "Sorry. Didn't mean to startle you. You okay in there?"

She didn't answer. Her lips moved, but no sound came.

"I'm gonna open the door, alright?"

He tried the handle. It wasn't locked. The door popped open with a click.

She flinched.

"Easy," he said gently. "I'm Deputy Jeremy Apps with the Lancaster Sheriff's Office. You're safe now."

She stared past him, over his shoulder toward the tree line. Her body was shaking.

"Ma'am," he said again, keeping his tone low. "What's your name?"

No answer. He took a step back and paused. "Can you come with me to the cruiser? It's warm. We'll get you somewhere safe."

It took several tries. He kept his voice calm and slow.

Eventually, she nodded and allowed him to help her out. As she stepped out, she grabbed her phone with trembling fingers, holding it close to her chest. Her knees wobbled, and he steadied her with one arm.

He led her gently to the patrol car and opened the passenger door. He retrieved a blanket from the trunk and draped it around her shoulders.

Once she was settled inside, he circled back to the red sedan, grabbed the keys from the ignition, and locked it before returning to his cruiser.

He grabbed the radio.

"Dispatch, this is Deputy Apps. I've got a female subject, late twenties, picked up about five miles outside Lancaster. Car was parked roadside. She's conscious, appears in shock. I'm bringing her in for medical evaluation."

There was a crackle before dispatch responded. "Copy that, Apps. Proceed to county hospital. They've been notified."

Jeremy clicked off the radio.

The woman was curled into the seat, holding the blanket tight. Her face had gone pale now that the shock was wearing off, but she still wasn't speaking.

He kept his eyes on the road. "You got a name?"

A pause.

"M... Mallory," she whispered.

"Nice to meet you, Mallory. You out here by yourself?"

She didn't respond right away. Then, with a stammer, she said, "V-victor. My husband. He... he was with me."

Jeremy nodded gently. "Where is he now?"

She struggled with the words.

"A m-monster... in the woods. Took him."

Jeremy kept his voice even. "Alright. We're gonna get you checked out first. Let's take it one step at a time."

She said nothing else the rest of the drive.

When they reached the hospital, Jeremy helped her inside. Two nurses rushed over with a wheelchair and ushered her to a triage room. A doctor soon followed. They spoke softly to her, got her seated, and began the process of running basic tests. Shock was setting in hard. They checked her temperature, blood pressure, and ran a few neurological tests. She barely spoke and didn't resist anything they did.

Once she was admitted and sedated, Jeremy lingered at the nurses' station, filling out a basic report and passing along her name.

Out in the cold again, he pulled out his phone and called Blackridge's Sheriff, Ben Beretti.

The call was answered after two rings.

"Sheriff Beretti," came the gruff voice.

"Sir, this is Deputy Apps from Lancaster. I picked up a woman on Highway 5. Said a monster took her husband. She was sitting alone in a car, still in shock."

There was silence on the line.

"Where exactly?"

"About five miles outside Lancaster. Her name's Mallory Bellinger. She's been admitted. They're doing some tests, but she's not in any shape to talk more tonight. I thought I'd let you know, given the creature issues you've had recently in Blackridge."

Beretti sighed audibly. "Thanks Deputy Apps. I'll send Agents Beretti and Jacobi your way in the morning."

Jeremy nodded, wind rustling around him. "That's probably wise. We'll have a search team out for her husband at daylight."

"Understood," the sheriff said.

He ended the call and stood in the parking lot for a few moments longer, watching the wind scatter dry leaves across the pavement.

Whatever Mallory had seen had shattered something in her. He'd seen that look before, but only on soldiers.

And that chilled him more than the wind ever could.

CHAPTER 26

The sun had barely crested the hills when Beretti pulled the black FBI-issued SUV off the shoulder of Highway 5. She and Jacobi stepped out, the morning wind biting through their jackets. The flashing blue and red lights of two Lancaster cruisers lit the roadside in soft pulses. A third unmarked SUV and a uniformed truck were already there.

"Lovely way to start the day," Jacobi mumbled, rubbing his hands together.

Beretti didn't respond. Her eyes were on the scene ahead. A taped-off section about seventy yards into the forest, just past the ditch. Several officers moved along the treeline, one of them talking quietly with a man in plain clothes.

As they approached, a deputy looked up and straightened his posture.

"Agents," he said. "Deputy Jeremy Apps."

"Special Agent Beretti," she replied, extending a hand. "This is Special Agent Jacobi."

They shook hands all around. Jacobi offered a polite nod. "We appreciate the call."

"I figured Sheriff Beretti would want you both out here. Especially after what the woman said."

"Mallory Bellinger," Beretti confirmed.

Apps nodded grimly. "You'll want to see this."

He turned and led them toward the trees. The ground here was still damp from rain earlier in the week, soft and dark beneath their boots. Birds chirped occasionally, but even that seemed muted.

"There were footprints leading this way," Apps said, pointing toward the deeper forest, "and a short blood trail following the same path. From the spacing and angle, it looks like whatever it was ran parallel to the road for a while, then stopped. After taking the body, it walked off into the trees."

They passed two felled trees and came into a small clearing marked off with yellow tape. A metallic smell hit them immediately. Distinctly coppery.

"Over here," Apps said quietly.

He crouched beside a tree root and lifted the edge of a white sheet.

The head lay beneath it, turned slightly to one side, eyes open, mouth slack. A smear of blood trailed behind it like a short tail. The expression was blank, but the skin around the eyes had frozen mid-terror. A smashed DSLR camera sat a few yards away, the lens shattered, body cracked and muddy.

Jacobi crouched, his eyebrows raised. "Jesus."

"Victor Bellinger, I take it?" Beretti asked.

Apps gave a short nod. "It's all we found. No body. Just this."

Jacobi stood and scanned the perimeter.

"We're still waiting on the crime scene techs and the county coroner," Apps said.

Beretti and Jacobi stepped over to where the footprints and blood drops led into the deeper forest. The footprints were deep, nearly twice the size of a man's boot, with clear toe definition in the mud.

"Still fresh," Jacobi said.

Beretti nodded once, face unreadable. "We're heading to the hospital next. Has Mallory said anything else?"

"She was near catatonic last night," Apps said. "Only words she gave me were her name and that a monster took her husband."

Beretti looked at the forest one more time before turning back toward the SUV. "Let's see if she's ready to talk now."

"Thank you, Deputy," she added with a nod.

****

The hospital was quiet when they arrived. A nurse met them at the front desk and led them to a small room on the second floor. Mallory sat in a chair beside the window, knees pulled up toward her chest, arms wrapped around herself. Her hair was pulled into a messy bun, and her eyes were red and raw. A tray of untouched food sat on the side table.

The nurse leaned in. "She's stable. Still shaken. Didn't say much overnight. You can try."

Beretti stepped forward and crouched beside her. "Mrs. Bellinger? My name is Nicole Beretti. I'm with the FBI. This is my partner, Agent Jacobi. We just want to ask a few questions. Would that be alright?"

Mallory blinked slowly. She looked down, then back at them. Her voice was hoarse.

"I already told the police it took him. He's gone."

Beretti nodded gently. "We understand. We're just trying to piece together exactly what happened. Anything you remember could help us."

Jacobi stood off to the side, his posture relaxed, letting Beretti take the lead.

Mallory swallowed hard. "We were on the road. Headed north. Taking our time. Victor... he liked road trips. Said it helped him think."

She looked down at her hands, thumbs pressing into one

another.

"He thought he saw something. Like… a person, maybe? Someone tall, moving through the trees. That's what he said, anyway." Her voice was unsteady, words trembling around the edges. "I hadn't seen anything. But he… he had to check. He always needed to see for himself."

Her voice cracked. She closed her eyes and took a breath, steadying herself.

"I stayed in the car. He grabbed his camera and said he wouldn't be long."

Beretti waited a few seconds. "And then?"

Mallory's lips trembled as she tried to form the words.

"He walked out into the woods. It wasn't far, I could still see him the whole time. He thought this stump might've been the thing he saw running. He was staring at it like he wasn't sure if it had moved."

Her face twisted, pain rippling across it.

"It stood up."

Jacobi took a step forward. "What did?"

She didn't look at him. Her eyes were distant.

"The stump. It… stood up. Like it had just been sitting there, waiting."

Beretti kept her voice gentle. "And what did it look like?"

Mallory glanced at her, blinking quickly.

"It was tall. Covered in dark hair. And built, like a body-builder, sort of. But... off. Its arms were way too long. And its face, God, its face, it looked... twisted. Just full of rage."

She shook her head, wiping at her cheek.

"It looked at him as if it despised him. Not just wanted to kill him, but hurt him. Like it hated him just for existing. I could feel it."

"What did it do?" Beretti asked.

Mallory pulled in a shaky breath. "It ran at him. So fast. He didn't even move. He just stood there. I think... I think he was frozen."

She swallowed, tears spilling freely now.

"It grabbed his head. Just... grabbed it and pulled."

Her voice broke completely. She curled forward in the chair, a low sob catching in her throat.

Beretti stood and gave her a moment. Jacobi turned toward the door, waiting silently.

After a minute, Beretti placed a card on the table. "Thank you for talking to us. If you remember anything else, or just need someone to talk to, you can call us."

Mallory nodded without lifting her head.

They turned to leave.

"Ma'am?"

Beretti stopped and looked back.

Mallory sat up slightly, her eyes glassy and unfocused.

"It had red eyes," she said softly. "Evil red eyes."

Beretti said nothing. She just gave a quiet nod.

And then they left.

****

Outside the hospital, Jacobi climbed into the SUV and exhaled slowly.

"She saw Red Eyes."

"Sounds like it."

Jacobi looked over at her. "It sounded opportunist."

Beretti's hands tightened on the wheel.

"Sure did. The guy walked straight up to him without even knowing."

They pulled out of the lot and drove in silence.

Far behind them, through the hospital window, Mallory sat alone.

Still staring at the woods.

****

They headed back to the scene, grabbed their rifles, and followed the tracks.

They'd walked nearly a mile beyond the point where the last tracks had faded, pushing deeper into a part of the forest that felt older, thicker. The air had changed too, cooler and still.

Jacobi moved a low branch aside and let it swing back gently. "You notice anything missing?" he asked, his voice low.

Beretti paused, sweeping her gaze across the woods. "No birds. No rabbits. No deer. Even the insects seem to be gone."

Jacobi gave a small nod. "Dead quiet. I don't like it."

The silence wasn't just the absence of sound. It felt like something was breathing down their necks, watching. Every step they took felt just loud enough to break something invisible.

They pushed forward through a tight patch of young pines. Beretti held a branch aside for Jacobi, who ducked under it with his rifle still slung across his chest.

"Smell that?" he said suddenly.

Beretti lifted her head and sniffed. The odor was faint at first, but unmistakable. Thick. Musky. Like damp fur and something left out too long.

"Yeah," she said. "Not fresh, but strong enough to hang."

Jacobi stepped over a fallen log, sweeping the brush ahead of him with a slow glance. "Old scent maybe. Something bedded down around here."

They moved slower now, following the trace of the smell like it was a trail itself. Thirty more yards in, Jacobi stopped and motioned.

"Here," he said.

Tucked behind a wall of thick brush, barely visible unless you were standing right in front of it, was a hollowed-out space beneath a tangle of low boughs and deadfall. The canopy of woven limbs overhead had been arranged in a way that almost formed a dome. It wasn't random. The sticks and branches were bent and fitted together intentionally.

Beretti crouched. "Clearly not natural."

Jacobi stepped closer. "Big enough to lie down in. Easy."

He pulled back one of the lower limbs and peered inside. The interior was dry. The floor of the space had been cleared of debris. Packed down with pine needles and moss.

"A shelter," he said. "Kept dry too. Look at how the cover above is angled."

Beretti didn't say anything right away. She moved carefully, checking the way the outer branches had been fitted together. She touched several of them, running her hand over the surface of the wood, feeling how the fibers were bent but not broken. Whoever made this had taken their time.

Jacobi crouched again, glancing around the perimeter. "You think this was Red Eyes?"

Beretti gave a small nod. "Or one of them. This wasn't tossed together last night either. This has been here a while."

Jacobi took a few steps beyond the brush and knelt. "Got something else."

She walked over and saw the bones. Not a lot of them, but enough to make her pause. A forelimb maybe, too long for a rabbit. Maybe a deer, or something smaller. It had been cracked open. Hollow. Licked clean.

Jacobi stood and exhaled. "This place gives me the creeps."

Beretti scanned the woods again. "Whatever used this, they knew how to stay hidden. This is the kind of thing you don't find unless you're looking for it."

Jacobi nodded. "And maybe not even then."

They stood there for a long moment, listening.

The wind pushed lightly through the trees above, but down where they stood, nothing moved.

Beretti checked her watch. "We should head back."

Jacobi stepped away from the bones and gave the brush one last glance. "Yeah. Okay."

They turned and started retracing their steps, the sense of unease lingering like a fog around them. The silence never lifted. The birds didn't return. The woods watched them go.

CHAPTER 27

The creature moved through the forest with purpose. His arms swung low, fingers brushing tree trunks and tall ferns as he passed. The trail was known to him. Worn over seasons, it twisted through shadow and root, leading to the place where he rested, hidden from the eyes of the hairless ones.

He had left not long ago, dragging the broken body of the last one to a place deep between the rocks. The kill had been deliberate. He had known the male would come close, bold in his foolishness. He had waited with breath still and muscles coiled, then unleashed his rage in silence. The head had been discarded, left behind for others to find. A warning.

The body was his.

Now he returned to rest.

But the moment he crossed the ridge above his resting place, he stopped. The air was different. Wrong. It held the scent of the forest, yes, but twisted through it was something else. Two hairless ones had passed through. A male and a female.

He inhaled again.

The male's scent meant nothing to him.

The female's did.

He stood still for a long moment. The scent tugged at something deeper than instinct, reaching into buried memories. It was familiar, unsettlingly so.

She had returned. The girl.

She had been small when he first saw her. Hair the color of dry grass. Skin pale like river-stone. Her voice had drifted to him on the wind, high and strange. She had played in the dirt, spoken to animals, touched flowers without breaking them. He had watched her from the edge of the field, from the darkness behind trees, every night, and many days. She had laughed once, and it had stirred something in him he could not name.

But the older ones, her keepers, had kept her from him. They had taken her inside when he crept too close. They had locked her away in the wooden walls and covered her with noise and light. They feared what they could not see.

She had not been there the day he made her keepers pay for keeping her away from him.

That day was fast and brutal. When it ended, their voices were gone. He had searched for her, expecting her scent to rise nearby. He followed the river. He climbed the hills. But she was nowhere. Her scent faded with the rain, and after many turns of the moon, he stopped looking.

Now it was here.

He moved forward with a strange mix of curiosity, excitement, annoyance and caution.

His resting place was hidden beneath thick brush woven by his own hands. Leaves packed tight, branches bent and layered until they held strong. He ducked beneath the edge and entered.

It had been disturbed.

His bedding, shaped by years of repetition and weight, was no longer the same. The weave had shifted. The leaves no longer held his scent alone. He knelt, pressed his fingers to the place she had touched. Her hands had rested there. Her breath had warmed this space.

She had walked where he slept. Crouched in his silence. Taken in what was his.

The anger came quickly. Hot, sharp, alive in his chest. But beneath it, confusion. Curiosity. A stirring he had buried long ago.

Why had she returned?

She should not have found this place. Should not have known to come here. Yet her scent lingered like a question with no answer.

He turned and stalked out of the hollow. The rage needed somewhere to go. It clawed at his insides, wild and burning. He found an eight-inch-thick tree and gripped it hard, rocking it back and forth, driving the fury through his limbs. Each movement was harder than the last until the roots tore loose and it crashed to the ground. The sound echoed through the trees, but it gave him no peace.

Her turned to find her trail. It wound through the forest in a path she believed was unseen. He could smell her at every turn. Her steps were quiet, but not afraid. She had moved with care, not panic. She had come to study, not to flee.

He followed.

The trees bent over him. His shoulders brushed trunks and branches, but he did not slow. Each breath pulled her scent deeper into him. The memory of her face, once faint, had returned in full. She had been small. Pale. Eyes wide with wonder. A voice like birdsong.

But she would not be the same.

She had grown. Changed. Yet the scent was still hers. Still tied to what he remembered.

He pressed forward, following the trail she had left behind. The path bent between old trees and sloped toward a hollow where the light never reached. He moved without a sound, without pause.

The girl he had once watched had come back.

He needed to see her.

And when he did, he would decide whether she still belonged to the memory of what once was, or whether she had become like the rest of them.

CHAPTER 28

The paint roller slid up the wall with a satisfying sound, smooth and even. Beretti leaned into it, arm moving in long strokes, lost in the rhythm. Jacobi stood nearby with a brush, trimming the edges where the dining wall met the ceiling. The smell of fresh paint filled the air, sharp and clean, mixing with faint dust and the scent of old wood that no amount of scrubbing could erase.

They had been working all night. Over the Christmas break, they had been staying with Ben and Leoni in town, but some nights they drove out here to the old house to work on it. The place needed attention. Walls were patched, floors cleaned, the roof finally sealed. New doors and windows had been installed. Ben had picked up the hammer again after too many years of letting it sit. Said it was time the place came back to life. Leoni helped often, cleaning and packing meals. With Jacobi's help too, the place was finally coming together.

This was Beretti's childhood home. Every corner held a shadow of the past. Every creak of the floorboard tugged at something buried.

Tonight had been quiet. They'd eaten sandwiches for dinner,

sitting cross-legged on the floor while paint dried around them. Ben had taken over the bathroom to fix the plumbing, mumbling about corroded fittings and whoever installed them decades ago. Leoni had gone down the hall to tackle the back bedroom. She wanted to clean out the closet before painting started in there.

Jacobi stepped back and examined his handiwork.

"Straight lines," he said. "You're welcome."

Beretti smirked. "Don't get cocky. That corner's crooked."

"Crooked?" He squinted at it. "That's art."

She laughed. "Right. Right"

Whiskey and Wink were curled on the tarp near the entryway, little bellies full from the last bit of roast Ben had slipped them earlier. The dogs had followed Leoni at first, but settled here after she disappeared down the hallway.

It was peaceful.

Until the dogs lifted their heads at the exact same moment.

Wink gave a single sharp bark and shot to his feet. Whiskey didn't bark. He growled, low in his throat, their hackles up.

Beretti froze. Jacobi lowered his brush and turned toward the door.

"They do that often?" he asked quietly.

Beretti shook her head. "No."

Whiskey's body was completely stiff, ears pointed forward. Wink gave a nervous whine and backed up behind a paint can.

Jacobi stepped toward the window, scanning the dark outside. "Movement?"

"I don't see anything," Beretti said, crossing to the entryway. She set her roller down and reached for the rifle she had leaned against the corner earlier. She picked it up and chambered a round without hesitation.

From the hallway, Ben's voice echoed out. "What's going on?"

"Dogs are acting off," Jacobi called.

They heard the click of a toolbox being set down and then footsteps. Ben came around the corner with a rag over one shoulder and his sidearm holstered at his hip. He glanced at the dogs and didn't bother asking again. He unholstered the gun as he moved past them.

Whiskey and Wink both stared at the front door, growling in unison.

Heavy footsteps began to rise up the porch steps. Slow, heavy, each one groaning against the wood.

Beretti raised her rifle, heart pounding. She flicked off the safety and took aim. Jacobi moved to her side with his side arm ready, eyes narrowed.

Ben positioned himself near the wall. "Leoni?" he called.

"I'm in the back," she answered, a little breathless. "Why?"

"Stay put."

The porch creaked again. Something massive shifted its weight just beyond the door.

They could hear it breathing. Low and thick, with a rasp that rattled like whatever it was had massive lungs. A shadow stretched across the front window, bulky and motionless.

Beretti stared at it, breath tight in her chest. Jacobi shifted beside her, gun tracking with the silhouette's movement.

The door handle jiggled.

Wink yipped and scrambled backward. Whiskey growled louder but didn't move from his place.

Beretti steadied her aim. Jacobi's eyebrows lowered.

The handle turned again. Just a small rotation. Testing.

They could hear it sniffing. Slow breaths drawn in at the gap near the doorframe. It moved slightly, sniffed again, then paused.

The dogs didn't move. Neither did anyone else.

Footsteps creaked away across the porch. Two. Three. Then nothing.

Beretti didn't wait.

She strode forward, rifle tight in her hands.

"Nicole," Leoni called from the hallway, voice tense. "Don't... shouldn't you wait?"

Beretti didn't respond.

She threw open the front door.

The porch was empty.

She stepped outside. The air hit her all at once, sharp and cold, and laced with a stink that made her eyes water.

It was heavy. Musky. Like fur matted with damp earth and rotting trash. It clung to the railing and floorboards, a trail that led toward the edge of the property.

She crouched and scanned the ground, rifle ready.

Jacobi followed, sidearm raised, sweeping left and right. "Anything?"

"No," she said.

"We know that stink well," Jacobi said as he screwed up his nose.

She stepped off the porch and onto the driveway. The air felt heavier out here, still and watching. She looked around the property. The trees beyond the edge of the lot stood motionless in the dark, the space between them thick with shadow.

No sound. No movement. But she knew he had come and gone.

They stood on the gravel drive a minute longer before turning back.

Inside, Leoni had already made coffee. She handed Ben a mug, then poured for the others without speaking. The dogs had retreated under the dining room table and didn't come out.

No one said anything for several minutes. They drank and sat still, eyes darting toward the door every time the wood creaked.

Ben finally broke the silence. "You think that was Red Eyes?"

Jacobi nodded. "I'd bet on it."

Beretti set her mug down. "Yes."

Ben looked over at her. "Did you know he would?"

She frowned. "Why would I know that?"

"Because you kept that rifle close," he said. "You don't usually do that unless you're expecting trouble."

Jacobi leaned forward. "You touched his bedding. You walked all over it. You knew he'd remember your scent."

Beretti hesitated.

"I thought it was possible," she said. "But I didn't think he'd come this quickly."

Ben gave a short shake of his head. "But he did."

Jacobi stared at her. "You baited him."

"I didn't plan to," she said. "But yeah. I gave him a reason. And now I know."

"Know what?" Leoni asked, voice quiet from her chair.

Beretti looked down into her mug. "He remembers me."

Leoni's brow furrowed. "From all the way back then?"

Beretti nodded. "He watched me when I was a kid. For weeks. I didn't know it at the time. But now I do. He saw me then, and now he knows I'm back."

Ben sighed. "So what now?"

Beretti stood and walked to the window. She pushed the curtain aside and stared out at the dark.

"I use it," she said. "I make him come to me."

"And then what?" Jacobi asked.

"Then we see who walks away."

CHAPTER 29

The moon was bright enough to read by, not that Looselips Larry was in any hurry to crack open a book. He had other priorities. His legs pumped the pedals of his beat-up green Schwinn, the squeaky chain keeping rhythm with his own off-key whistling. He balanced a half-smoked joint in the corner of his mouth, the cherry flaring with each inhale.

He was a sight, no doubt. Long gray hair tucked under a faded LSU cap, an army jacket that probably hadn't been washed since Y2K, and a pair of mismatched gloves, one fingerless, one not. A big scar split his left eyebrow from a bar fight he didn't remember starting. His pants were duct-taped at the knees, and a roll of toilet paper bounced from a carabiner clipped to his belt loop.

Larry had been on the road for years, drifting from one small town to the next, earning his nickname back in New Orleans when he snitched on the wrong crew and had to disappear. He'd tried to keep his mouth shut after that, but old habits died hard. These days, no one paid him much mind, and he liked it that way. He lived for two things: weed and wheels.

He was used to the dark. It didn't scare him. When he was tired, he just pulled out his old swag and rolled it out wherever he liked. He had slept in culverts, empty barns, on top of picnic tables, and once, in the bed of an abandoned truck. He'd fought off a cougar in Utah and a rabid raccoon behind a bowling alley in Oregon. He wasn't afraid of much.

Tonight, both the weed and the wheels were cooperating.

He coasted along Highway 5 just past Blackridge, belly full of microwaved noodles and a gas station energy drink that tasted like melted bubblegum. On his left were open fields, covered in silver moonlight. On his right, the woods huddled in tight clusters, black and watchful.

He whistled louder, a tuneless melody that only made sense to him, and took a long drag on the joint.

"Hot damn," he muttered, exhaling through his nose. "Ain't nothin' like a moon ride with a fresh spliff and empty road."

The fields to his left rippled slightly. Grass moved against the still air. He glanced over, more curious than cautious.

At first, he thought they were deer. Two shapes, low and wide, heads down in the grass.

Then a third stood up. And a fourth.

He slowed the bike and squinted into the moonlight. The figures weren't graceful. Their movements were jerky, impatient.

"Wolves?" he mumbled. "Nah. Too clumsy."

He pedaled a little farther and looked again. There were

five now.

"Dogs?"

The figures raised their heads at the same time. Ears perked.

Larry's bike squeaked again, and the shapes twitched. Then they started running.

Straight toward him.

He blinked, took the joint from his mouth, and watched the pack close the distance with terrifying speed.

"Oh, hell no."

He ditched the bike mid-roll, one foot hitting pavement as he sprinted across the road. His legs weren't what they used to be, but fear lit a fire under him like nothing else could. His boots slapped against the bitumen, lungs struggling to keep up.

Behind him, barking exploded, raw, snarling, and vicious.

"Leave me alone!" he shouted over his shoulder. "I ain't got nothin' but arthritis and attitude!"

The road blurred underfoot. He spotted a tree just off the shoulder, thick enough to hold him and low enough to grab. He didn't think. He jumped.

Fingers caught the lowest branch, and somehow, through sheer desperation, he hauled himself up, one grunt at a time.

"Come on, come on, come on."

The dogs hit the tree moments later, barking like they were possessed. They snarled and leapt, jaws snapping inches below his boots.

Larry climbed higher, about ten feet up, wedged himself between two thick limbs, and clung to the trunk like it was the last safe place on earth. His chest heaved.

The joint was still between his fingers.

He laughed, breathless. "Still got it."

He took a shaky puff and looked down.

The dogs were circling the base, eyes shining in the moonlight. A mutt with torn ears paced left and right while a thick pit mix growled low, teeth bared. One looked like a Rottweiler and some other mangy combination. Another had wiry fur and a limp. The last one was small but fast, zipping around the others like a scout.

"Well y'all sure are enthusiastic," Larry said, trying to catch his breath. "What'd I ever do to you, huh? I'm just a man. A man with noodles in his belly and no clue what day it is."

He exhaled smoke down at them, which did absolutely nothing.

"Alright," he said, voice softening. "Let's all calm down. No need for all this commotion."

The dogs didn't calm down.

"You ever just sit and watch a sunset?" he asked them. "Ever think about how weird corn looks up close? Life's got better things than gnawin' on folks, I promise you that."

Still barking. Still leaping.

Larry leaned his head against the bark and sighed.

Then, without warning, the barking stopped.

All five dogs turned in the same direction. Ears up. Bodies rigid.

Larry blinked and sat up straighter. "What now?"

The dogs stared into the field. Then, one by one, they ran. No hesitation. No final snarl. Just gone. Vanished into the moonlit grass like they'd never been there.

Larry stared after them, his mouth half open.

"Well... that's new."

He looked around. Nothing moved. The wind was still.

"Guess I bored the hell outta them."

He chuckled and took a final drag from the spliff, then held it up like a toast.

"Here's to quiet nights and bad dogs."

He flicked the ash and watched it fall. The cherry hit a patch of leaves and burned for a second before going out.

A crow landed in a nearby tree and squawked a few times.

Larry looked up at it. "Well hello there. Nice to make your acquaintance. What's your name?"

The bird flapped its wings and took off without a reply.

"Well, that's rude," Larry mumbled.

He was just about to swing his leg down and start climbing when he caught a nasty scent. Strong. Rotten.

Larry screwed up his nose. "Is that me that stinks?"

He sniffed under his arm.

In that instant, something yanked him backward.

No warning. No sound. Just raw force.

The joint slipped from his fingers.

As his back hit something solid and cold, he turned his head in time to see a face. Not a man. Not a dog. Something else entirely.

Two red eyes stared into his.

Looselips Larry managed one last word, drawn-out and hoarse.

"Fuuuuuuck."

The woods swallowed the sound.

And then he was gone, never to be seen again.

CHAPTER 30

Beretti was up before the others. The sky had only just begun to shift from deep blue to soft gray, and the town of Blackridge lay still beneath the quiet of early morning. The only sound came from the occasional groan of old pipes warming in the walls and the soft rustle of the dogs shifting on the bed.

She stood on the front porch of Ben's place with a hot mug in her hands. Steam curled into the cold air and vanished before it reached her face. She didn't sit. Just leaned against the railing, eyes scanning the street and sky.

Her thoughts were sharp. Rest hadn't helped. If anything, it had made the night before settle deeper. The memory of the scent outside the old house still clung to her. So did the sound of something massive moving on the porch. She could still feel the tension in her muscles when she opened the door and found only air.

She had never truly believed he would come to the old house. Not this quickly. Not without hesitation. But he had.

The door creaked behind her.

Ben stepped out, a steaming mug in his hand. He wore a jacket over his uniform shirt and gave her a quiet nod as he joined her at the railing.

"Morning," he said.

"Morning."

They stood there for a while in companionable silence, watching the slow brightening of the horizon.

He sipped from his mug. "So... what are you going to do once you take care of Red Eyes?"

Beretti didn't look at him. "What do you mean exactly?"

"I mean, I worry that all this searching, all this time spent chasing him but not catching up... maybe it's been a way of holding on to the past. Once it's done, it's done. Nothing left to chase. It's all in the past then."

Beretti turned the mug slowly in her hands. "I hadn't really thought of that. Honestly, I've just been focused on finding him. Going over the reports. Checking the sightings. It's been nonstop the last few weeks."

"I get that. I do. I just worry about you."

She gave him a soft smile. "It's okay. Really."

Ben gave a small nod. Just as he was turning to head back inside, his phone rang.

He pulled it from his pocket, answered with a quiet "Sheriff

Beretti," and listened for a moment. His expression changed.

He hung up and looked at her. "Someone's traveling bike was found abandoned on the side of Highway 5. It's under Lancaster's jurisdiction but they want me to check it out."

"Need our help?" she asked.

"From the sounds of it, there's not much to go on. I'll call you if I need you."

She nodded. "Okay."

Ben gave her a look that said he'd keep her in the loop, then disappeared back inside.

A few minutes later, the door creaked again.

Jacobi stepped out barefoot, coffee in one hand, hair a wreck, and a sweatshirt half on. "You ever sleep?"

"A little," she said.

He joined her at the railing, took a sip, and squinted at the quiet street. "You think he will stay around the old house now?"

"I think it's possible."

Jacobi nodded, his mouth tight around the rim of the mug. "Me too."

They stood in silence while the light grew. The cold seeped into their fingers, but neither moved. A few birds began calling from the trees, and a pickup rumbled a few blocks over, too far to matter.

Jacobi finally said, "You still up for the ridge above your old place?"

Beretti looked over at him. "Of course."

They got ready, grabbed their rifles and headed out of town just after sunrise. The drive was quiet. They passed frost-covered ditches, long stretches of barbed wire, and fields that looked brittle under the early light. The old mailbox near the turnoff still leaned sideways. Nothing moved beyond it.

Jacobi drove with one hand on the wheel, enjoying the early morning scenery. Beretti drank from a fresh cup of coffee, her eyes on the shifting rows of trees outside.

They backed in beneath a stand of pines, the SUV nestled in shadow. Frost coated the grass and needles around them, and the air stung their cheeks. There were no tracks on the trail. No broken branches. Not even deer sign.

Jacobi unloaded the drone case and laid it open on the tailgate.

"You mind?"

Beretti shook her head. "Go ahead."

He unpacked the equipment, humming a Taylor Swift song as he unfolded the drone's arms and checked the mounts.

Beretti noticed but said nothing. She'd save that one for another day.

He handed her the spare tablet once everything was linked and confirmed.

"You're my second set of eyes," he said.

Beretti took it and stood a few feet off, rifle over one shoulder, eyes on the screen as the drone lifted.

It rose smoothly and hovered. Jacobi guided it forward and angled the camera down toward the slope and the tree line beyond.

They scanned in silence.

Nothing moved.

No deer. No birds. No signs of anything alive at all. The forest looked emptied out, as if every creature had scattered hours before.

Beretti narrowed her eyes. "Too quiet."

Jacobi adjusted the feed. "He's probably here somewhere then."

He took the drone lower, weaving carefully between the branches. The feed showed dark trunks, dried leaves, and underbrush that didn't stir.

Twenty minutes passed.

Then something caught her eye.

"Stop. Go back."

Jacobi moved the drone back a few yards and hovered.

Near a downed log, half-shadowed beneath the edge of a hill, sat a shape that hadn't been there before. It looked rounded. Still. Possibly a stump.

Then it shifted.

Beretti leaned forward. "There."

A small rock flew past the drone, fast.

Jacobi didn't flinch. "He sees us."

"Back it out," Beretti said.

"Just a second."

Another rock snapped past, closer.

"Jacobi."

He angled the drone lower.

"What are you doing?"

"I want to be sure."

The drone crept in beneath a branch, just over the log.

The figure lifted.

Broad shoulders. Cracked gray-black skin. A deep scar split the upper lip. Heavy brow. And the eyes. Red. Fixed on the drone with full awareness.

Jacobi whispered, "It's him."

A rock flew straight at the camera. The feed jerked, flickered, then cut to black.

Beretti lowered her tablet. "You ding dong, Jacobi."

He stood motionless, staring at the screen. "What?"

"That drone cost fifty thousand dollars."

He winced. "Yeah. Sorry."

"I told you to pull it back."

"I just wanted to make sure it was him."

Beretti slung her rifle around and started walking toward the vehicle. "Well, now we know. And now we don't have a drone."

Jacobi followed, closing the case. "My bad."

CHAPTER 31

The sun was low when they pulled up to the old house. The surrounding field faded into cooler hues, earth-toned and quiet. Beretti stepped out of the cruiser, coffee in hand, her breath faint in the air.

She walked the perimeter slowly, brushing against fence posts, letting her presence settle into the ground. At the porch, she stepped deliberately on every board leading up to the front door, her boots heavy and loud. She touched the railing, the frame, the handle. Inside the doorway, she took a few extra steps in and out, just to be sure.

"Making sure he knows where to go?" Jacobi asked from behind her.

Beretti looked back over her shoulder. "If he comes, I want him looking here."

"You're setting the stage."

"Exactly."

They went inside. The place felt even older than usual in the late light, all worn floorboards and hollow quiet. Jacobi laid out their dinner on the table, sandwiches from the last open diner in town. He handed her one without speaking, and they sat.

She drank first, then unwrapped her sandwich. Roast beef and swiss on rye. Still warm.

"You really want to do this?" Jacobi asked.

Beretti nodded. "Yeah."

He leaned back a little. "Once you get an idea in your head, you don't let it go, do you?"

"No," she said. "I don't."

He smiled, but it didn't quite reach his eyes.

Outside, the wind picked up slightly, brushing against the windows. The temperature was dropping fast. Later winter meant clear skies, sharp nights and just enough warmth in the day to make it bearable.

Beretti zipped up her jacket. It was soft, fleece-lined, and silent when she moved. She pulled her black beanie over her ears, tucked every strand of her blonde hair up and out of sight. Her face was already marked with black paint, smeared in rough lines along her cheekbones and jaw, a streak across her nose.

Jacobi eyed her as she checked the strap on her sidearm. "You look like you're going to war."

She pulled out her night vision goggles from the duffel and clipped them to her belt for now. "Feels like it."

He followed her outside as she grabbed the blanket and the rifle from the back seat. The ladder was already in place, leaning up against the low slope of the house.

"You good?" he asked.

"Yeah."

Beretti climbed carefully, each rung taken with precision. The ladder groaned but held firm under her weight. When she reached the top, she stepped onto the roof and crouched low. Jacobi didn't wait. He moved the ladder and laid it flat in the grass behind the house.

She set up in the same spot they had discussed earlier in the day, on the forward-facing slope just above the porch roof. She unrolled the blanket and lay down on her stomach. Her rifle rested in front of her, sidearm still at her hip. The goggles were adjusted and set, flipped up for now.

She pressed her chest against the blanket, elbows tight, and adjusted the small radio clipped to her collar.

"Check," she whispered.

Jacobi's voice came through clear. "Loud and clear. You're good."

"Copy that."

She could hear him step back inside. A few seconds later, he keyed in again. "I'm at the kitchen table. Got the TV on low, just enough to make it look like someone's home."

Beretti didn't respond at first. She was watching the field, her eyes moving across the treeline.

The roof was cold but manageable. Sixty degrees, maybe just under, with the wind cutting low across the shingles. It was steady, not gusty, which was good. She settled in and let her breathing slow.

The forest around the property was still. Moonlight touched the tops of the trees, enough to cast soft contrast once her eyes adjusted. It wasn't full moon bright, but it was enough. And she had the goggles if needed.

"You good up there?" Jacobi's voice came quiet over the radio.

"Yeah. It's peaceful."

"That's always the setup for something awful."

She smiled faintly. "Maybe."

A long pause followed.

"Still can't believe you wanted to sleep on the roof tonight," he said.

"Who said anything about sleeping?"

Jacobi chuckled. "Fair."

She checked the safety on her rifle, not touching the trigger, just reassured by the motion. Then she adjusted slightly, tucked her head down, and let her senses stretch outward. No movement in the trees yet.

"You remember that case in Nevada?" Jacobi said, breaking the silence again.

"Which one?"

"The one with the lake. That thing with the gills and the long fingers that kept stealing bait buckets from the docks."

Beretti snorted. "Oh yeah. The fisherman who thought it was his cousin messing with him."

"Until he saw the handprint on his cooler."

"With webbed fingers."

Jacobi nodded. "Still convinced it was messing with him on purpose. Took only the good stuff, too."

Beretti smiled. "You only like that one because it never tried to kill us."

"I like any cryptid that doesn't scream and charge at me. Low bar."

"You also tripped on that guy's tackle box."

"I was testing reflexes."

"You landed in a pile of worms."

He shrugged. "It was strategic."

Beretti let out a soft breath, eyes still on the scope. "You're lucky no one filmed that.”

“I bet someone did.”

She didn’t answer right away. The wind moved through the trees, steady and cool. “I’d still go back there.”

Jacobi nodded. “Same. Chill cryptid. Good sandwiches.”

A few minutes passed. Crickets chirped. Dry leaves rattled in the branches above. The night held its breath.

After a long pause, Beretti said, “So... Taylor Swift, huh?”

Jacobi blinked. “What are you talking about?”

“You were humming the song earlier today.”

“Oh. Hahaha. Yeah, that song always gets stuck in my head.” He sang, off-key, “Glad to meet you where you’ve been.”

Beretti chuckled. “Okay, enough.”

A cool breeze blew through and rustled some leaves.

Beretti looked toward the sound without moving her head. No other movement.

Thirty minutes passed.

Jacobi checked in again, quieter this time. “Still good?”

“Still watching.”

“I’ve got your back,” he said.

"I know."

She didn't say more. There wasn't anything else to say.

Out in the field, the trees shifted slightly with the breeze. The grass moved in slow waves. The sky above held a quiet silver sheen, just enough to outline the shapes below.

Beretti stayed still.

Watching.

Waiting.

CHAPTER 32

Ally was only in town for a few nights. She and Jamie had gone to college together before Jamie met her boyfriend Damian and moved out to the county. It had been months since they'd seen each other in person, and this visit was meant to be an easy catch-up. Just two friends, some wine and a quiet night in.

They pulled into the driveway and Jamie shifted the gear into park. The porch light glowed ahead, spreading pale light across the gravel. Trees framed the property like a jagged crown, dark and unmoving.

Jamie opened her door and stepped out, the cool air brushing against her skin.

Ally hesitated. "It's dark out here."

Jamie grabbed her bag from the passenger seat. "That's what happens when you live in the country."

Ally finally climbed out but stayed close to the car. "I'm serious. I don't like it. I swear I heard something in those trees."

Jamie closed the door and walked around to her. "Relax. We're home."

They started toward the house as the wind picked up just enough to rustle the low brush near the edge of the yard.

A sudden snap echoed from the treeline.

Both women froze.

Ally grabbed Jamie's arm. "What the hell was that?"

Jamie turned, eyes scanning the dark. "Probably the wind."

"That was not the wind." Ally's voice rose in pitch. "Jamie, I don't like this."

Another sound followed. Louder this time. A heavy, rhythmic crashing like something moving fast through the woods. Something big. Coming straight for them.

Jamie's eyes widened. "Okay, go. Get to the porch."

They ran, but Ally's boots slid in the gravel and she fell hard, landing on her side with a sharp cry.

"Ally!" Jamie doubled back without hesitation, grabbing her under the arms. "Come on, get up. We gotta move."

Ally scrambled to her knees, breath hitching. "It's coming, I hear it."

"I know. I know. Come on." Jamie pulled her to her feet, half dragging her toward the steps.

Another branch snapped, closer now, followed by the unmistakable sound of something charging through thick brush.

Jamie hauled Ally up the steps, heart hammering. Her fingers trembled as she fumbled with her keys, flipping through them with frantic hands.

"Jamie, please...open it, please," Ally cried, voice shaking.

"I'm trying. Fuck. Fuck. Fuck."

"Open it!"

"I've almost... hang on."

"Hurry, Jamie!"

Jamie shoved a different key into the lock and twisted hard. The door opened, and both women fell inside in a scramble. Jamie kicked the door shut and locked it.

For a few seconds, nothing.

The porch creaked.

Ally crouched on the floor, arms wrapped around herself. "What was that?"

Jamie crawled to the window and peeked through the curtain, her breath catching. "There's nothing there."

"What?"

Jamie sat back on her heels. "Nothing. Guess it was a deer or something."

Ally stood, jittery. "That was not normal. That was not an animal. That was... I don't know what the hell that was."

Jamie stood, trying to steady her own breath. "Maybe a bear?"

Ally shot her a look. "No way. That was too fast. Too loud."

Jamie didn't respond right away. Then she let out a shaky breath and gave a small laugh. "God. We probably looked ridiculous."

"You did," Ally said, grabbing the wine bottle from the kitchen counter. "But I won't hold it against you if you pour me a glass."

Jamie smiled and stood. "Deal."

They settled into the lounge room, curtains drawn, wine glasses in hand. They watched a reality show, full of dramatic music and over-the-top arguments. Gradually, their tension eased.

An hour passed.

Then two.

Jamie curled up on the couch, hoodie pulled tight, phone in hand.

Ally lay on the beanbag, one sock half-off, texting and laughing under her breath.

Jamie's phone buzzed. She glanced down. "Damian. Says he's staying in Redding tonight. Got a hotel near the aged care place."

Ally looked up. "Is his mom doing better?"

"Yeah. They had a good visit, and he wants to see her again in the morning before heading back."

Ally nodded. "That's good."

Jamie stood and stretched. "I'm gonna take the bins out before I forget."

Ally wrinkled her nose. "Right now?"

"Yeah. They're nearly full, and I don't want to miss the pickup."

Ally waved her off. "Fine. I'll fill our glasses while you're gone."

Jamie pulled her hoodie tighter and grabbed the trash bag from the kitchen before heading to the door.

Outside, the air had cooled. No breeze. No insect noise. Just a thick, pressing stillness.

She stepped off the porch and moved around the side of the house, the trash bag swinging at her side.

The bins waited near the fence line. She mumbled, "Should've made Ally grab the other one," and yanked the heavy wheelie bin out into the open.

The driveway stretched ahead, empty and quiet.

Jamie tugged the bin toward the road, glancing once over her shoulder. Nothing moved. She kept moving.

Two sharp squawks cut through the silence. She jumped at the sound then laughed nervously when she realized it was just a crow.

"Shit. You scared me," she mumbled, dragging the bin forward.

The wheels thunked over a patch of gravel. A small stone caught under one of them, and she had to yank it harder to keep it moving.

She passed the edge of the porch light and stepped into shadow.

Her hand shifted on the handle. The bin felt heavier than it had a minute ago.

She glanced toward the road. Just a few more steps.

Behind her, the trees shifted.

Something moved.

Something fast.

Something heavy.

The sound came hard and sudden. Pounding footsteps. Branches breaking. A roar of movement.

She barely had time to turn.

****

Ally paced the living room, eyes darting to every shadow the muted television light couldn't reach. Jamie had just stepped outside, trash bag in hand. She'd said it casually, even smiled, clearly not as rattled as Ally still was.

But Ally hadn't forgotten. Not the crashing sounds. Not the feeling of something barreling toward them in the woods.

It had taken hours for her heartbeat to settle.

She checked the time. Jamie had been outside for over five minutes. It didn't take five minutes to put out a bin. Even if she was texting Damian or dragging it around the side of the house, it shouldn't take this long.

Ally stood at the door, peering through the narrow window. Nothing moved out there. The porch light was on.

She bit her bottom lip, hesitant, and called out.

"Jamie?"

No answer.

Her stomach flipped.

What if whatever was in the woods earlier had gotten her?

Should she call 911?

But what if Jamie was just struggling with the bin, or dropped the bag? What if she called, and they came out for nothing and she looked like an idiot?

She opened the door just a little and leaned out.

"Jamie, you good?"

Still nothing.

"Shit."

She grabbed her phone from the coffee table, turned on the flashlight, and stepped outside.

The porch light cast a faint glow onto the gravel, but it didn't reach the trees. The driveway was longer than most, typical for a country property, and Ally stayed close to the house, sweeping her light over the area near the porch.

"Jamie?" she called again, her voice thinner now. "You better not be messing with me."

She took one step down, then another. The gravel crunched beneath her sneakers. Her light landed on the trash bin, upright, lid closed. Bag was inside.

But no Jamie.

"Why do you have to live out in the boonies?"

She walked slowly past it, light bobbing with her steps. The beam touched something pale near the end of the drive.

She froze.

Her flashlight trembled in her hand as she aimed it again.

Jamie was lying on her side, one arm twisted beneath her,

eyes wide open.

Ally blinked fast, not understanding what she was seeing at first.

Then she saw the post.

The wooden letterbox post, torn from the ground, was lodged through Jamie's head. Blood-soaked the gravel beneath her. The mail was scattered like confetti in a horror show.

Ally let out a sharp scream and stumbled back.

She turned and ran into the house, slamming the door behind her and locking it. Her breath came fast and loud. She ducked behind the kitchen bench, the phone shaking in her hand as she tried to dial. Her fingers fumbled so badly she nearly dropped it. She had to crouch low and steady herself before trying again.

When the dispatcher answered, Ally was already crying.

"There's been a murder... someone's killed my friend... please send someone... Enterprise Road... I don't know the number... I don't know the number..."

"Okay, calm down, ma'am," the dispatcher said gently. "You're doing great. Can you check a piece of mail or something nearby for the house number?"

Ally spun around, frantic. She ran to the hall table and grabbed the first envelope she saw.

"Seventy-nine," she cried. "Seventy-nine Enterprise Road."

"Help is on the way," the dispatcher said. "Stay inside. Lock the doors. Don't go back outside for any reason."

Ally backed away from the door and sank to her knees, rocking slightly, unable to stop shaking and crying.

****

Red and blue lights flickered across the trees as Sheriff Ben Beretti's truck skidded to a stop in front of the house on Enterprise Road. Two deputy cruisers were already parked at odd angles near the drive, and an ambulance idled nearby, its interior light glowing faintly. One of his deputies approached as Ben stepped out, the concern already plain on his face.

"Scene's cold," the deputy mumbled, angling his light across the driveway. "Still and quiet."

Ben gave a single nod and walked toward the body, now covered with a blanket one of the first responders had gently placed. He crouched beside it, eyes scanning the overturned trash bin and the flutter of loose mail near the base of the driveway.

He peeled the blanket back slowly.

The girl's face was still visible, though slack. Her head was twisted too far, unnaturally. Her neck had been broken and the mailbox post driven clean through the back of her skull, pinning her to the gravel. Her jaw hung open, blood crusted between her teeth. The kill had been immediate. Efficient. Savage.

A younger deputy came up behind him, swallowing hard. "Sheriff... you think a local did this?"

Beretti didn't answer right away. He looked back down at the body and then turned toward the deputy.

"Unlikely," he said. "Given the young lady's head is facing the wrong way, and the fact the mailbox had been cemented into the ground."

The deputy paled and stepped back. "Yeah... ok."

Another deputy walked over, radio in hand. "The friend's still inside with the first responders. She's shaken but okay, said she saw the body when she stepped out to check on her. So far, that's all we've got."

Beretti nodded. "I'll talk to her in a few."

He turned his gaze to the treeline. The woods were quiet. Still.

This hadn't been a break-in or a lover's quarrel. It wasn't the work of some sick individual looking to make a name for himself.

Ben was almost certain it had been a Sasquatch.

And more than likely, it was Red Eyes.

He pulled out his phone and tried calling Nicole.

Straight to voicemail.

Tried Jacobi. Same result.

He clicked his tongue and slipped the phone back into his pocket.

"We need photos. Mark the blood spatter, check for tracks, keep the perimeter tight," he said to his deputies.

They nodded and got to work, flashlights bouncing as they moved into their positions.

Ben lingered for another moment, staring down at the girl. Her body was still. The post unmoving. The wind picked up slightly, rustling the edges of the trees.

He exhaled slowly.

Wherever that thing was, it wasn't going to stop of its own accord.

CHAPTER 33

The rooftop was colder than before. Beretti pressed her cheek against the stock of her rifle, the soft blanket underneath barely insulating her from the chill that had crept into her bones. The wind had calmed but not died, just enough to keep her alert.

She blinked, long and slow, resisting the pull of sleep. It had been hours.

Her muscles ached. Her fingers were stiff, though not numb. She hadn't shifted in too long, and her body was reminding her. She couldn't move now. Not unless she had to.

To keep herself awake, she let her thoughts drift, only a little.

She remembered a morning when she was five, bundled in her favorite blue coat, running through the frost-covered grass behind the house, her mother's laughter drifting from the porch. Her father had been stacking firewood by the shed, pretending not to notice her trying to sneak up behind him. She had yelled and pounced. He scooped her up like a feather, swinging her around while she squealed.

She smiled at the memory. Then another one followed.

The same backyard. Different season. Her mother crying in the kitchen after a phone call. Her father sitting on the edge of the bed, staring at the floor, not saying a word. The tension in the house had been a presence then, thick like smoke.

Beretti closed her eyes for a moment and opened them again.

What would life have been like if they'd lived?

Would she have gone into law enforcement? Would she still be chasing shadows in the woods?

She pushed the thoughts away. Now wasn't the time to fall into grief or regrets. Her mind had wandered long enough.

The clock on her wrist read just after four in the morning.

She breathed in slowly.

A foul odor drifted on the breeze.

Her nostrils flared before her brain even caught up. It came in faint but clear.

Musky. Damp fur or hair. Wet dog. Faint traces of rot beneath it.

She didn't move.

Her head remained still, cheek pressed to the rifle. But her eyes shifted left, then right, scanning the field, the tree line, the porch. She listened hard.

The insects had gone quiet.

No wind now. No rustling. No owls or distant yips from coyotes.

Just dead silence.

Like a vacuum had dropped over the property.

He was here.

Her thumb clicked the radio softly. "He's here," she whispered.

Inside, Jacobi had been nodding off in the kitchen chair. At her voice, he startled upright, heart hammering.

He fumbled for his rifle and crossed to the front window. Then the back. Eyes sharp now. He pressed his mouth to his radio. "Copy. No movement outside. I'm watching both sides."

Beretti stayed still, breath measured, ears straining.

Minutes passed.

Nothing.

A long, drawn-out call drifted through the trees.

"Niiiiiiiiiiiiiiiiiiiicooooooooooooooooooooooooole..."

"Niiiiiiiiiiiiiiiiiiiiiicoooooooooooooooooooooooole..."

She froze.

The voice wasn't right. It had shape, a cadence. But it was

wrong in the details. Stretched. Too low at the start, then rising unnaturally at the end.

Like someone trying to say it without ever having formed the word before.

Again.

"Niiiiiiiiiiiiiiiiiiiiicooooooooooooooooooooooole…"

Jacobi's voice came over the radio. "That is not creepy at all."

Beretti didn't respond.

She had heard it. Loud and clear. Her name.

It wasn't just mimicry.

It was memory.

He had heard her parents call her that. Maybe in the yard. Maybe through a window. He had watched. He had listened. And now he was playing it back, like some warped recording looping in the dark.

Her stomach turned.

She scanned the trees. Nothing moved.

Then, without warning, laughter.

It began as a high-pitched giggle. Piercing. Too fast.

It rose and twisted mid-sound, turned scratchy and loud, up and down in cadence, like a child imitating laughter but without rhythm or reason. It screeched in places, rasped in others.

It lasted too long.

Thirty seconds.

Beretti clenched her jaw and pressed closer to the roofline, resisting the urge to cover her ears. Her eyes darted through the darkness, searching for any shape that didn't belong.

Inside, Jacobi stood frozen near the front window, rifle in hand. He had never heard anything like it.

He whispered into his radio. "Beretti... you still have eyes?"

Her hand clicked the radio. "Still nothing."

He waited a beat. "That laugh... I felt that in my spine."

"Yeah," she whispered. "Same."

The silence returned.

Even heavier than before.

The air felt thicker. The cold more present.

Beretti's finger hovered near the trigger. Her breath fogged the edge of the scope but cleared again before she had to wipe it.

She stayed like that for the next hour.

Eyes peeled. Body tense.

Watching.

But Red Eyes never stepped out of the tree line. Never entered the field. Never made another sound.

The scent eventually faded, but her pulse didn't.

****

At sunrise, the horizon bled gold and gray across the tops of the forest. The light softened the corners of the house and made the frost on the grass shimmer.

Jacobi stepped out the back door, quietly, and repositioned the ladder.

Beretti didn't move until he called out, "All clear. Come down."

She lowered the rifle, flipped the goggles off, and took a long breath.

Her muscles ached as she rose to a crouch and shuffled to the edge. She descended slowly, rung by rung, her body stiff from staying in one position too long.

Jacobi met her at the bottom.

"You alright?"

She nodded. "Yeah. Sore, but alright."

They stood in silence for a moment. Beretti stretched her

limbs as they talked, rolling her shoulders, flexing her fingers, and working out the stiffness in her legs.

"Do you think he saw you?" he asked.

"I don't know," she said. "Maybe. Maybe not."

Jacobi studied her face.

"But he didn't show himself," she added. "And that pisses me off."

Jacobi gave a small nod. "You think it was a game?"

"No," she said. "It was a message."

He raised an eyebrow. "And what did it say?"

"That he remembers everything."

CHAPTER 34

The shrill buzz of her phone dragged Beretti from a restless sleep. She blinked against the late morning light leaking through the window, her arm groping the nightstand until she found the phone and turned it over.

Ben's name lit the screen.

She sat up immediately. "Hello?"

"Sorry to wake you," Ben said. His voice was tight, no small talk. "We've got a situation. Young girl's gone missing."

Beretti was already throwing back the blanket. "Where?"

"Outskirts of town. Her mom saw it happen about an hour ago. She said a gorilla took her kid and ran into the trees."

Beretti froze with one foot on the floor. "She said gorilla?"

"Yeah. Not a bear. Not a man. A gorilla."

She was on her feet now. "Text me the address."

"Already did."

She ended the call, moved quickly to the door, pulled it open, and called out, "Jacobi!"

He answered from the next room, groggy. "What?"

"We've got a missing child. Outskirts of town. Kid was taken right in front of her mother."

There was a pause. "Taken?"

"She said a gorilla took her."

He appeared in the doorway already pulling on a shirt. "Well. Shit."

They dressed quick without speaking. Beretti pulled her hair back, and they took turns in the bathroom, grabbed their rifle bags, and met by the front door.

Ten minutes later, they were on the other side of town, speeding toward the address Ben had sent.

As they pulled up to the property, the scene was already active. More sheriff's cruisers were lined up along the gravel drive, along with several civilian vehicles parked at awkward angles near the edge of the field. Deputies were spread out across the property, some clustered near the treeline, others organizing search teams.

A woman stood on the porch of the small farmhouse, speaking with a deputy. She was dressed in jeans and a sweater, her hair pulled back in a tight braid, hands shaking as she gestured toward the forest. Her face was puffy and etched with concern.

They had just opened the cruiser doors and were pulling their rifle bags from the back seat when Ben spotted them and walked over.

"Before we get into it," he said, "we had another incident last night."

Beretti straightened. "What happened?"

"A woman was killed out on Enterprise Road. I tried to call you both, but your phones were off."

"Sorry," Beretti said. "We were doing a stakeout at the old house. I only turned it back on just before we crashed."

Ben gave a brief nod. "It was bad. No question in my mind it was him."

"Enterprise Road?" Jacobi asked, his brow tightening. "That's where Craig Dalton's brother lives, right? We spoke to Craig a few days ago."

"Yeah. It was his brother's girlfriend who got killed. I'll fill you in properly later."

They stood silent for a beat before Ben gestured toward the woods. "We've got two teams already scouring the area in both directions. No signs yet."

Beretti nodded, scanning the treeline. "What's the terrain like?"

"Mixed. Thick woods east, open pasture to the north, but the girl was taken toward the treeline behind the barn. No cameras."

"Have you got a photo of the girl?" Jacobi asked.

Ben pulled out his phone, tapped the screen a few times, and held it out to Beretti.

She stopped mid-check when she saw it.

A blonde girl, maybe eight years old. Long hair. Big smile. A little gap between her teeth. Her eyes were wide, bright blue, and curious.

Beretti felt the breath catch in her throat.

She looked like her.

Not just vaguely. Not like any little girl might. She resembled Nicole Beretti at that age. Hair the same length. Smile tilted the same way. Even the nose. Even the shape of the jaw.

Ben was watching her face. "Yeah," he said quietly. "I thought the same thing."

Jacobi leaned over to see the photo and froze. "Damn. That's unsettling."

Beretti kept her eyes on the screen a moment longer. "What's her name?"

"Jasmine," Ben said.

They finished checking their rifles, slung them over their shoulders, and joined the nearest search group, working their way into the forest.

They moved single file through the thickest part of the woods. Deputies called out the girl's name every few minutes, but the only response was wind moving gently through the trees.

Beretti scanned up and down as they moved, watching for broken branches, scuffed leaves, drag marks. Anything.

But there was nothing.

No blood. No tracks. No trail.

The woods felt empty.

Hollow.

Jacobi walked beside her, rifle slung across his back, his expression grim.

Three hours passed. The sun moved higher, the light sharper now through the bare branches. The birds had returned, chattering here and there, and squirrels darted across the ground in bursts.

But there was no sign of the girl. Or what took her.

Beretti eventually stopped near a rotting log and sat down hard. She wiped her forehead and let out a long breath. Jacobi stood nearby, watching her.

"You alright?"

Beretti nodded but didn't speak right away. Her eyes were fixed on the ground.

Jacobi lowered his voice. "We're not gonna find her here, are we?"

She looked up at him, her jaw tight. "No. We won't."

"Why?"

Beretti exhaled through her nose. "Because I think I know where he would've taken her."

Jacobi knelt beside her. "Where?"

"My old house."

He stared at her, searching her face. "You're sure?"

"My gut says that's where she is."

Jacobi didn't hesitate. "Then let's go."

They stood and turned back the way they'd come, cutting through the trees with purpose now, moving faster than before. As they neared the road, Beretti clicked her radio.

"Ben, it's Nicole. Jacobi and I are heading out. I've got a strong lead."

Ben's voice came back, short and direct. "You need backup?"

"Not yet."

"Keep me updated."

They reached the cruiser, climbed in, and shut the doors. Jacobi started the engine and threw it into gear.

"You think he took her because he couldn't get to you?" he asked, eyes on the road.

Beretti stared straight ahead. "Maybe. Or maybe he took her because she looks like I did."

Jacobi didn't respond.

They drove in silence for a few minutes, both of them locked in thought.

Beretti's fingers tapped restlessly against her knee.

"If he's using her to draw me out," she said finally, "then he knows exactly what he's doing."

Jacobi nodded slowly. "Then let's make sure he regrets it."

CHAPTER 35

She had not seen him. But he had seen her.

From the shadows near the edge of the field, just beyond the human dwelling, he crouched low, still as stone. His breath was steady. His eyes did not blink.

He watched the small one run between the trees, her long yellow hair catching the morning light. The sound of her laughter tugged at something buried deep.

It was not just the way she moved.

It was who she was.

She lived there. He could smell it in the earth, in the leaves she crushed underfoot. He had circled the property for two nights. He had smelled her on the toys, on the swing, on the stones near the creek.

She belonged here.

But what struck him most was how much she looked like the other one. The one he had watched years ago. The one who reminded him of everything that had been taken from him.

She had not chosen to come with him then.

And now, she had returned.

At first, he thought it meant something. That she returned for him. That she understood.

But she had come to kill him.

Not to join him. Not to understand him.

The rage blinded him.

She would pay for that.

He would make sure of it.

The child in the yard ran to her female keeper. He could hear them speak, though the words made no sense. The tone did. The mother's voice was light, distracted. She had no idea he was near.

He crept low through the underbrush. A fallen limb cracked, but the mother only looked behind her for a second before turning back to the house.

That was the moment.

He moved fast.

From the trees to the girl.

His arms wrapped around her like steel. She cried out once, but it was cut short by the speed of his retreat. Her legs kicked, but he was already gone, her voice swallowed by the woods behind them.

The female keeper screamed.

It echoed through the air, loud and useless.

He did not slow. Not when the girl writhed. Not when she bit his forearm. Not even when her cries turned to sobs.

She was not the one he wanted.

But she would bring the one who was.

He moved through the forest, deeper, always turning, always hiding the path. She was small and light, though loud. He growled once, and she went still, her little hands gripping his hair with terror.

He knew exactly where to take her.

The dwelling that belonged to the yellow-haired girl.

The place he had returned to again and again, long after the others had gone.

He had walked up to where the hairless ones came and went, their scent no longer strong.

He had stared through the clear wall, watching for movement inside.

He had sniffed the steps where her feet once landed.

He had waited there more nights than he could count.

Now, he would wait again.

But this time, she would come.

Not as a child. Not with innocence.

She would come with fire in her hands.

And when she did, he would be ready.

CHAPTER 36

The cruiser flew down the back road, tires eating up the distance between town and the old house. Beretti sat forward, eyes locked ahead and focussed. Jacobi gripped the wheel tight glancing now and then at Beretti. Neither spoke.

They didn't need to.

The moment the house came into view, a tight knot of nerves coiled in Beretti's chest.

Jacobi parked fast and reached for the latch.

Beretti was already out.

They moved around to the back of the cruiser and each retrieved their rifles from the rack. Jacobi started to follow her to the field, but Beretti stopped him with a hand to his chest.

"Let me do this," she said quietly.

Jacobi looked at her. "What do you mean?"

"I need to go out there alone."

His face tightened. "No way. We go together."

Beretti shook her head. "I have to be the one. He took that girl because of me."

Jacobi stared at her, torn.

"If this goes bad," she continued, voice low but steady, "you're on the porch. Cover me from there."

Jacobi looked past her toward the field. "You're sure about this?"

She nodded. "Yeah. Just wait for my signal."

He didn't say anything else. Just pressed his lips together, then turned and jogged toward the porch, positioning himself behind the post with a clear view of the field.

Beretti stepped forward alone.

The field was open, wide, and quiet. The grass moved gently in the wind, but nothing else stirred. She walked slowly, her boots silent on the earth, the rifle hanging at her side.

She just walked.

Ten steps in, she stopped.

And waited.

She tried to steady her breathing, but her thoughts ran too fast.

What if he didn't come? What if she was wrong about everything? Standing alone in an open field, waiting for a monster. It felt ridiculous. Brave maybe, but also stupid.

It's fine. Jacobi has my back.

Still, the anxiety pressed against her ribs like a second heartbeat.

Had he hurt the girl? Left her somewhere to die?

No. If she was right, if he had taken her because she looked like her as a child, then maybe he hadn't.

Get your shit together Beretti. You've got this.

The sounds of the forest buzzed around her, birds calling in uneven bursts, a woodpecker tapping somewhere farther off. The breeze blew through the pines with a soft sigh.

Twenty minutes later, it stopped.

All of it.

Like someone had hit a switch.

Dead silence.

Beretti's pulse quickened, but she didn't move. Her breath came slow. Her body stayed loose. Her hand rested lightly on the rifle's grip but didn't tighten.

She stared into the tree line.

A crow landed on the roof of the house, squawking loudly in the silence. Beretti lifted her hand slowly, palm up in a calming gesture. The crow tilted its head, then flapped its wings and flew off.

Seconds passed.

Then minutes.

The tension crept across her shoulders, tightening with every step. She didn't dare shift her footing. Her heart pounded so hard she could feel it behind her ribs.

A shadow peeled out of the trees. Massive. Towering.

More than nine feet tall.

He stepped forward without hesitation, heavy limbs moving with the power of something that had no fear. His arms hung low, his frame thick with muscle beneath the matted hair.

And his eyes.

Red.

Piercing.

Almost hypnotizing in their intensity.

They burned across the field and locked onto her, pulling at something deep inside. The sight of him nearly took her breath away. The surge of old emotions hit her harder than she expected. Fear. Anger. Grief. Anxiety.

He held the girl in one arm.

She was awake.

Her face was pale, but she wasn't crying. She looked at Beretti across the field, her eyes wide, lips slightly parted. She didn't speak. She didn't scream.

She just watched.

Red Eyes stopped just beyond the first row of trees. His breathing was heavy but even. His gaze pinned Beretti in place with impossible focus.

Across his face was recognition, rage, and dark glee.

He raised his free arm slowly, palm half open.

A low grunt rumbled from his chest, not loud but clear.

Without taking her eyes off him, Beretti crouched and set the rifle down beside her, the barrel resting gently in the grass.

From the porch, Jacobi whispered, "What the hell are you doing?"

Her hands stayed open.

She took a step forward.

Red Eyes did the same.

The girl still didn't move. Her eyes shifted between the two of them like she knew something important was happening but couldn't explain it.

Beretti walked one more step closer.

The wind picked up, brushing her jacket back, and lightly

blowing strands of hair across her face.

She didn't show any fear.

She just stood there.

So did he.

And the standoff began.

CHAPTER 37

Beretti stood motionless in the middle of the field, the rifle lying beside her in the grass. Her arms hung loose at her sides. Jacobi crouched on the porch, one knee braced against the post, rifle ready. His heart hammered as he watched her, knowing this could go wrong in a thousand ways.

Beretti swallowed and took a slow breath. Her voice was calm but firm.

"Let her go."

Red Eyes stood still, breathing heavy. His eyes, bright red and intense in the afternoon light, never left Beretti. They had a strange ancient-like pull to them.

"You came for me," she said. "Not her. Let her go."

Still nothing.

She spread her arms slightly. "I'm here."

No movement.

Jacobi's eyes flicked between them. He could see the girl in Red Eyes' grip, unmoving, her small frame partially obscured. He had never been more afraid to pull the trigger, or more terrified not to.

An idea struck Beretti. Maybe it wasn't just the words. Maybe it was the language. She tried again, this time in Karuk.

"Áama iicháari." *(Don't hurt.)*

The words felt strange on her tongue, old and unused, but she said them with purpose. She saw something flicker in Red Eyes' expression. A shift.

"Yuták taav," she said gently. *(Girl, go.)*

His head tilted, eyes narrowing slightly.

Beretti took another step forward, speaking only in Karuk now.

"Tákun ta kunish táat." *(Leave the child alone.)*

"Káriiv vúra ni." *(Take me instead.)*

Red Eyes let out a deep grunt. His grip on the girl loosened, then tightened again. He seemed unsure.

Beretti kept going, her voice calm but firm.

"Áfyi vúra pay." *(Let this end now.)*

"Vúra kiríh." *(Just peace.)*

"Núf tá hiivúr." *(You hurt inside.)*

"Nú uríh tá kunish." *(I don't know why.)*

Something shifted.

Heat surged behind her eyes. Beretti flinched as a wave of images slammed into her mind. They weren't hers. They were his.

Frantic shapes moving through the trees. The chopping roar of something above. His mother running, wild-eyed. His father shielding her as blood sprayed. The look of terror on his sister's face. The Elder lying still, surrounded by blood.

She could feel his pain. His hatred. His loneliness.

The vision cut off as suddenly as it had come. She gasped, knees softening beneath her, but she kept her footing.

"Áta húutih." *(I'm sorry.)*

"Tá kunish náav ku." *(That wasn't me.)*

"Tá kunish u'yáam ta híih." *(You cannot kill the innocent.)*

She took another step forward.

"Áfyi vúra pay." *(Let this end now.)*

"Káriiv vúra ni." *(Take me instead.)*

"Nú tá kunish yuták." *(Let the young one go.)*

"Káriiv tiicháari." *(Walk to me.)*

He stood still for several long seconds.

Then, finally, he crouched down and placed the girl on her feet.

She hesitated.

Beretti pointed toward the house. "Run. Fast."

She bolted, feet pounding across the grass. Jacobi didn't take his eyes off Beretti or Red Eyes. Not even when the girl reached the porch. He said, "Sit down behind me and don't move."

She dropped behind him and sat down, beginning to cry softly.

When the child bolted, Red Eyes' attention snapped after her. Beretti seized the moment.

She reached slowly into her pocket, fingers brushing the small leather pouch. Her hands moved with care. She brought out the pepper seeds and palmed them. Then she brought her hand toward her face and faked a light cough, slipping the seeds into her mouth.

It burned immediately. Her mouth lit up with heat and her eyes watered, but she didn't flinch. Just tried to breathe through it.

Red Eyes turned his attention back to her.

"Nikáa ishkéesh." *(You knew my mother.)*

His expression sharpened.

"Nikáa peí." *(You knew my father.)*

His eyes brightened. His shoulders squared.

Then he charged, covering the 20-yard gap in a split second.

His hand closed around her throat and he lifted her into the air. He didn't squeeze. Just held her there, face to face, her feet dangling inches above the ground.

Jacobi's finger hovered over the trigger.

"Fuck. Wait, Jacobi. Wait," he whispered to himself.

Beretti didn't panic.

She stared into Red Eyes' face.

The memory of the last time she saw her mother and father waving to her flashed into her mind.

"You took my parent's lives," she whispered. "Now I'll take yours."

Then she spat.

The pepper juice hit him directly in the eyes.

He shrieked in pain and shock, dropping her immediately, hands flying to his face as he staggered back. He screamed, the sound wild and piercing.

Beretti rolled as she hit the ground, came up on her knees, and drew her knife in one fluid motion.

She charged forward and plunged the blade into the inside of his thigh, pushing hard and dragging until she saw the spray of blood.

Red Eyes shrieked, staggering and flailing blindly. One

massive hand caught her by the shoulder, fingers digging in hard as he yanked her upward.

Before she could react, a high-powered round slammed into Red Eyes' upper torso. The shot came from the porch.

He roared and dropped her.

Beretti got up quickly, breath ragged, and dove in again. She slashed at the other leg. The blade sank deep. She dragged it again, cutting into the second artery.

Red Eyes reeled, stumbling in circles, bellowing in rage and pain. He rubbed at his eyes violently, seemingly unaware of the blood pouring down his legs.

He took two steps sideways and fell hard onto his shoulder. The ground shook. He groaned and rolled onto his back with effort, his breaths coming in sharp, ragged pulls.

Beretti stood, slow and shaking. Her hands and clothes were soaked in blood. Her mouth was still on fire from the peppers.

She stared at him.

Jacobi moved from the porch, approaching slowly. He passed the girl without looking down and said, "Stay here. You're safe."

Beretti walked toward Red Eyes lying in the grass, chest heaving, arms twitching. He moved his eyes to find her as she stood over him.

He snarled weakly.

She didn't flinch.

"Jacobi," she said.

He came up beside her. "Yeah?"

"Your handgun, please."

He handed it over.

Beretti looked down at Red Eyes. "This is for my mother."

She shot him between the eyes.

"This is for my father." She shot him again, between the eyes or whatever was left of that area.

She lowered the gun, aimed once more. "And this," she said, "is for me." She fired between his legs, into his genitals.

Then she handed the weapon back to Jacobi.

A wave of emotion surged through her. Her body shook. She sank to her knees and began sobbing, hard and sudden, like something had broken loose inside her that had been held too long.

Jacobi stood nearby and said nothing. He just stayed close.

She knelt in the bloodstained grass, shoulders shaking, and let it all out.

It was done.

CHAPTER 38

Insects stirred in the grass, clicking and chirping as if they sensed it was safe to come out again.

A black SUV rolled in along the dirt path, followed closely by two matte-gray vans with government plates and no markings. The vehicles slowed to a crawl as they approached the massive, still body sprawled near the center of the field.

Beretti stood nearby, arms crossed against the chill, her breath visible in the fading light. Her voice was raspy, and sweat clung to her forehead despite the cold, lingering effects of the peppers. She wore the same clothes from earlier, stained, scraped, and heavy. Faint red marks circled her neck from his grip. The adrenaline was long gone. What remained was exhaustion and something deeper she hadn't quite named.

Jacobi stood beside her, his hands buried in his jacket pockets. His eyes moved to her arm, spotting the blood soaking through her torn sleeve where Red Eyes had dug his fingers in.

"You want the paramedics to take a look at that?" he asked quietly.

Beretti shrugged. "I can patch it up myself."

Then he noticed she still clutched her knife. The blade was streaked, her grip loose but steady.

"That knife came in handy," he said.

Beretti looked at it like she hadn't realized she was still holding it. "Yeah. My mother made it by hand. Gave it to me not long before she was killed."

Jacobi tilted his head. "What's that word on the handle?"

She brushed her thumb along the bone. "It means instinct. In Karuk."

"It's beautiful," Jacobi commented.

Beretti smiled faintly, wiped the blood from the blade onto her pants, then slipped it back into its sheath and tucked it into her pocket.

A clean-up team of eight men stepped out of the vans, all wearing white medical overalls. They moved efficiently without speaking. They worked around the creature's massive frame, rolling him carefully onto a thick, reinforced body bag. It took all of them working together to maneuver his limbs, muscles straining as they got him into place. The industrial-strength gurney had already been lowered flat to the ground, which saved their backs. Once secured, they hoisted the bulk of the bag up and locked the gurney back into position, built specifically for extreme loads.

Across the clearing, Sheriff Ben Beretti stood near a parked patrol cruiser. His stance was guarded, but the tension in his shoulders had eased. He was with the girl's parents now. Jasmine had been wrapped in a thick blanket, her head resting on her father's shoulder. Her mother held onto both of them, arms trembling but firm.

Ben had made sure the ambulance was waiting. Jasmine would be checked at the hospital, but she appeared okay. Shaken, pale, quiet, but safe.

Beretti's gaze shifted back to the tree line. It was still. The breeze whispered through the tall grass. No movement. No red eyes staring back.

Jacobi finally broke the silence. "You holding up?"

Beretti didn't answer right away. She just kept watching the team work.

"Yeah. Just... it's a lot. I'm a little overwhelmed."

He nodded once. "Of course you are."

She looked down at her boots. "I made an appointment."

Jacobi blinked. "For what?"

"With the Bureau's psychologist. The other day."

He tilted his head slightly. "Really?"

"Yeah. I figured... if I were dating someone, and they said they were seeing a therapist, or they said they weren't... I'd pick the one who was."

Jacobi let out a low, surprised laugh. "That's an interesting metric."

"Just makes sense to me. At least they're trying. At least they're honest about their trauma and what to live a better life."

He looked over at her, the fading light catching the edges of her face. "I think that's great. And I really hope it helps."

Beretti gave a small nod but didn't reply.

The gurney had a motorized base and all-terrain tires, designed for field retrievals. It groaned under the weight but inched forward, slowly but steadily, across the uneven ground as the men guided Red Eyes toward the open van doors.

Jacobi watched the process in silence. "Hard to believe something that powerful ended up like that."

Beretti said, "I'm just glad it's him and not one of us."

"You and me both," Jacobi replied, giving her shoulder a pat.

They stood in silence as the doors closed. When the last one clicked shut, Beretti felt a slow unwinding in her chest. Not relief. Not closure. But something.

Jacobi looked up at the darkening sky. "So... where to next?"

Beretti watched the vehicles preparing to pull away. "I'm sure there'll be another monster. Somewhere."

"There always is," he said.

"Let's hope the next one bleeds easier."

Jacobi cracked a faint smile. "Or is under nine feet tall."

Beretti gave a quiet snort. "That would be nice."

They turned slightly as the ambulance doors opened. Jasmine was passed gently into the waiting arms of a paramedic; the blanket still wrapped around her. Her mother followed close behind. Her father's eyes never left her, even as a medic began asking quiet questions.

Ben approached them and gave a steady nod. Nicole and Jacobi nodded back.

"Thank you," he said, looking at them both. "You guys are incredible. I mean that."

Jacobi gave a small smile. "It was all her."

Nicole shook her head. "We both saw it through."

The sun was almost gone now. The edges of the forest were dipped in purple, the air sharper with cold.

Jacobi rubbed his neck. "Honestly, a hot shower sounds amazing. Maybe even a stop at the local bar."

Beretti exhaled slowly. "That sounds great. Count me in."

They started walking toward the cruiser, as Beretti glanced around, noticing the air felt lighter.

Jacobi looked over at her. "Hey. What did you spit in his face?"

Beretti gave a faint, tired smile. "Ghost Peppers. I found them in the house the other day. I grew up on these things. Stuffed them in my pocket just in case. I didn't remember them until I was in the car."

Jacobi raised his eyebrows. "You were carrying peppers into battle?"

"Figured I'd use them if I got the chance. I wasn't even sure if they would still have a kick. But damn, they surely did."

He laughed quietly. "I'm impressed. That was smart. No wonder you're sweating."

Beretti looked ahead again. "We're fighting cryptids, Jacobi. We have to get creative."

They both smiled and kept walking.

She hadn't told him about the vision Red Eyes had forced into her mind, but she would. Just not tonight.

EPILOGUE

The house didn't creak anymore. It stood solid at the edge of the driveway, boards tight and clean, windows trimmed in fresh white, the porch extended and wide like it was always meant to be that way. The roof was fixed. The siding too. A porch swing hung from new chains, freshly installed and gently moving in the soft breeze.

Beretti stood in front of it, boots planted in the dirt, hands on her hips as she studied the home that once cradled her childhood and shattered it in the same breath. She had walked these grounds barefoot as a kid, run through the field chasing frogs, picked blackberries from the overgrown edges of the property. For years, the memory of this place had wrapped around her like a heavy coat she couldn't take off. But now?

Now it felt different.

Behind her, Jacobi leaned against the side of Ben's cruiser, arms folded and eyes on the house. Ben stood beside Leoni, one hand resting on her shoulder. Wink and Whiskey trotted near the edge of the yard, sniffing the corners of the porch and circling each other in quiet curiosity.

Jacobi stepped forward, looking up at the fresh trim, the

clean roofline, the porch rail that didn't lean anymore.

"The whole place feels lighter now," he said.

Nicole nodded. "It does. It really does."

She let the silence stretch. It wasn't awkward. Just full.

Ben walked over and stood beside her, close enough that their shoulders nearly touched. He reached out and pulled her into a soft one-armed hug.

"I'm proud of you, kiddo," he said. "Your parents would be proud of you too."

Nicole looked up at him and smiled, then dipped her head gently into his chest. He held her there a moment without saying anything else.

Jacobi joined them and glanced at the porch. "You never said what you've decided to do with the house. Now that it's finished."

Beretti followed his gaze. "I talked to ASAC Ward last week," she said. "Told him I couldn't sell it. Couldn't live in it full-time either. But I didn't want to just let it sit."

Jacobi nodded.

"So I pitched him an idea. I told him this place could be more than just mine. That maybe it could help other people too."

Leoni tilted her head. "How do you mean?"

Nicole turned to them. "I want to use it as a retreat. A recovery space. For agents. For survivors. For people who've seen things they can't explain. For anyone who needs somewhere quiet to land for a while."

Jacobi blinked. "That's actually brilliant."

"I told Ward it wouldn't be official. No signage, no red tape. Just a place off the books. Somewhere people can come when they're not okay."

Ben's expression changed. He looked at her with something deeper than pride. Something close to awe.

"Maybe it will be just the thing someone needs to get back on track," she said.

They all walked up the steps together. The porch was smooth and solid beneath their boots. Wink followed, tail wagging. Whiskey stopped to sniff a post, then clambered up slowly, tongue hanging.

Inside, the house was warm and simple. Fresh paint covered the walls. Light fixtures gave off a soft glow. A couch and two armchairs faced the stone fireplace. Bookshelves lined one wall of the living room, already half full. A framed photo of her parents sat on a side table. Another photo showed a young Nicole with Ben, both grinning and covered in mud.

They moved through the house at an easy pace. Each room was new but familiar. The kitchen had open shelves and mismatched dishes. A small round table sat at the center, with four sturdy chairs that Nicole had found second hand.

Leoni wandered into the back room. "This used to be your room, didn't it?"

Nicole nodded. "Yeah. Now it's a space to read or draw or just sit. Whatever someone needs it to be."

There were two guest rooms, each one neatly made. Nothing extravagant. Folded quilts. Soft light. One of them had a window that overlooked the field.

They ended up back on the porch. The sun was dipping below the horizon as the windows glowed warmly behind them.

Jacobi leaned against the porch rail and looked out. "You know," he said, "I always thought we'd burn this place down when it was over."

Nicole smiled faintly. "Me too."

"But this is better."

"Yeah," she said. "It is."

Ben and Leoni stayed a little longer, then said their goodbyes. Wink and Whiskey had to be called twice before they jumped into the truck. Leoni hugged Nicole tightly. Ben gave Jacobi a firm handshake, then pulled Nicole into another hug, his expression unreadable but full of meaning.

When their SUV disappeared down the road, Nicole, and Jacobi remained on the porch.

He looked over. "You staying the night?"

She nodded. "Just tonight."

"I'll stay too, if that's alright."

"I'd like that," she said.

They sat on the steps together, side by side. The stars emerged above them, one by one. The night air cooled, but not enough to push them inside. It was quiet and still, in the best way.

After a while, Nicole leaned her head against Jacobi's shoulder.

"We did good, didn't we?"

"Yeah," he said. "We really did."

And the house stood behind them, no longer broken, no longer haunted.

Just home. Ready to welcome whoever needed it.

ABOUT THE AUTHOR

Luka T. Jacobs, an author from the picturesque Illawarra region south of Sydney, Australia, is passionate about cryptids like Sasquatch and Dogman. She lives there with her partner and their dog, Finnigan.

Luka's love for animals and adventure fuels her storytelling. With a background in Graphic Design and Art, she adds a unique visual flair to her work. An avid traveler and explorer, she draws inspiration from the wild, eager to share her imaginative worlds with readers.

Stay connected and join the conversation! Follow me on Facebook to interact and share your thoughts, explore my books on Amazon, and visit my website for more information about my works and upcoming releases. Don't forget to sign up for my newsletter, you'll be the first to hear about new books, exclusive content, and special offers!

FB: https://www.facebook.com/lukatjacobs

A: https://amazon.com/author/lukatjacobs

W: http://www.LukaTJacobs.com

JOIN CRYPTID HORROR CENTRAL

Join my email list and get first access to new releases and download my **FREE** short story *"The Dogman of Coldwater Creek"*.

WWW.LUKATJACOBS.COM

Dear Reader,

Thank you for diving into my book amidst a sea of choices, it truly means the world to me.

If you enjoyed the story, I'd love it if you shared your experience with others and left a review. As an independent author, your voice helps bring these tales to life for more readers, and every recommendation makes a tremendous impact.

Thank you again for joining me on this journey.

I'm so grateful to have you as a reader!

SNEEK PEEK: FOREST OF THE SASQUATCH: THEIR TERRITORY, THEIR RULES

The forest breathed its ancient rhythm. High above, the towering pines swayed in the fall breeze, their needles whispering secrets carried through ancient shadows. Sunlight filtered through the dense canopy, dappling the forest floor in patches of amber and gold.

Hidden deep within the Superior National Forest, near Devil's Track Lake, where the trees cast the deepest shadows, lay a place untouched by humans, the clan's secret sanctuary.

Even the animals of the forest seemed to sense the boundary of this sacred ground, avoiding it entirely. Deer grazed near its edges but never crossed into its heart. Birds flew above the cliffs but rarely landed near the cave's entrance. The natural world seemed to understand what the hairless ones could not: this place belonged to the Sasquatch alone.

Thick, unyielding walls of thorny thicket and dense brush surrounded the area, growing so tightly together that even the smallest creatures struggled to pass through. Towering trees formed a natural barrier, their twisted roots and low-hanging branches weaving into an almost impenetrable maze. Beyond the thicket, a sheer cliff face rose abruptly from the earth, its jagged surface streaked with moss and lichen. At its base, hidden among boulders and shadows, was the entrance to a vast cave system, cool and damp, where the clan had lived for generations.

The caves were a place of safety, a haven where the family slept, gathered, and raised their young. Here, in this untouched wilderness, the Sasquatch thrived, living in harmony with the forest. But their peace was fragile. The hairless ones had grown bold, venturing deeper into the forest, leaving trails of destruction in their wake.

Aluk crouched low beneath the brush, his eyes glinting as he watched a pair of hairless ones far below. He and his brother Matto had left the sanctuary to patrol the edges of their territory, as they often did when the hairless ones grew too bold. What they saw now made Aluk's fists clench.

The two hairless ones had arrived in a roaring metal beast, its tires gouging deep ruts into the soft earth. They had parked it at the edge of a clearing, its bulk looming like an unwelcome guest. One of them, a tall hairless one in a bright orange jacket, was crouched over the lifeless body of a deer, its glossy eyes staring blankly into the dirt. The hairless one's hands were red with blood as he hacked at the carcass with a hunting knife, his movements rough and careless.

The second hairless one, stocky with a scruffy beard, stood nearby, gathering sticks. "Told you this spot was good," he said, his voice carrying across the clearing. "Nobody comes out this far."

"Think they'll notice one less deer?" the tall hairless one asked, his laugh sharp and grating.

Aluk growled softly, his breath steaming in the cool evening air. His eyes darted to the thunder stick lying in the dirt near the stocky one's feet. A weapon capable of death from a distance, one the clan had learned to fear.

The deer was theirs. The clan depended on these woods for food. The hairless ones had not only invaded their sacred ground, they had stolen from it.

Matto placed a hand on Aluk's shoulder, his claws brushing against the coarse hair there. Through gestures and images, Matto conveyed his thoughts: Hold. Wait. The Elder forbids this.

Aluk's response came in a flood of sharp, vivid images: the hairless ones' bloody hands, their trash scattering across the sacred ground, the machine scarring the earth. They destroy. They take. How much longer will we watch?

Matto hesitated. He shared Aluk's anger, but the Elder's warning rang in his mind. The Elder had long insisted on secrecy, on patience. But patience had not stopped the hairless ones from encroaching farther each year.

Hidden in the tree line, Aluk and Matto crouched, watching as the hairless ones built their red-breath. The breath licked high into the sky, casting flickering shadows on the trees. One of the hairless ones stood and stretched, letting out a loud belch.

"I'm gonna take a piss," he said, stumbling toward the forest's edge.

The men wrinkled their noses as an awful stench wafted toward them. It was rank and overpowering, like garbage left out in the sun for days, layered with a heavy musk that clung to the back of their throats.

"Geez, what is that smell?" one of them mumbled, turning his head away.

Aluk's massive body tensed. He glanced at Matto, who raised a hand in warning. The elder's unspoken message was clear: hold back. Watch, but do not act.

But Aluk's mind surged with defiance. He sent an image of the hairless ones laughing, their red-breath consuming the sacred ground, the machine scarring the earth. Enough.

As the hairless one staggered toward the trees, Aluk shifted silently from his vantage point, slipping through the thick underbrush. His movements were precise, his hulking frame ghostlike in the moonlight as he circled closer. The rustle of the leaves, the crack of twigs, sounds that would have betrayed a human, blended seamlessly with the forest's natural rhythm.

The hairless one stopped a few feet from the tree line, fumbling with his belt. Aluk waited, crouched just beyond the brush, his eyes locked on his target.

Before Matto could stop him, Aluk lunged forward.

The hairless one barely had time to gasp before Aluk's hand clamped over his face, silencing him. In one swift motion, Aluk dragged the hairless one into the thickets. There was a muffled cry, then silence.

Back at the red-breath, the second hairless one looked up, frowning. "Derek?" he called, squinting into the darkness. "Quit screwing around, man."

He heard a faint rustling from the direction Derek had gone. Then, the snapping of branches. A silhouette moved at the edge of the firelight, massive and looming, too large to be anything human.

A wave of panic washed over him, accompanied by a deep, unsettling fear. He stumbled back toward the clearing, nearly tripping over his own feet. His eyes darted around, trying to pierce the blackness. "Derek?" he called again, his voice trembling now.

When no response came, he turned and sprinted toward his four-wheeler parked near the fire. His hands fumbled as he started the machine, the engine roaring to life. The noise echoed through the forest, jarring and unnatural.

"Not sticking around for this crap," he mumbled, his voice

shaking as he gripped the handlebars and gunned the throttle. The four-wheeler lurched forward, kicking up dirt and leaves as it sped down the narrow trail towards the clearing's edge.

The trail was dark, lit only by the pale beams of the machine's headlight. The hairless one's pulse quickened, the trees seeming to converge, their shadows alive with an unseen, unsettling presence. He glanced over his shoulder, expecting to see something chasing him.

As he glanced back at the trail, his eyes widened in disbelief.

Standing in the middle of the path was a towering figure, its hair gleaming faintly in the four-wheeler's headlights. The creature's glowing eyes locked on him, and its massive form blocked the trail entirely.

"Jesus Christ!" the hairless one screamed, shifting his weight as he jerked the handlebars in a frantic attempt to avoid the creature.

The four-wheeler skidded out of control, its tires losing traction on the dirt. The hairless one's panic made him overcompensate, and the machine careened off the trail. It slammed headfirst into a tree with a sickening crunch, the force throwing the hairless one forward.

His body hit the tree with brutal force, a sharp thud reverberating in the woods. He crumpled to the ground at its base, groaning in pain. Blood poured from a deep gash on his forehead as he tried to crawl away, but his body betrayed him, too stunned to respond.

Aluk and Matto emerged silently from the darkness.

The brothers towered over the injured hairless one and the machine that had defiled their sacred forest. Aluk's lips curled back in a snarl as he sent an image to Matto: the machine broken, destroyed, its noise silenced forever.

Matto stepped forward first, his massive hands gripping the four-wheeler. With a guttural roar, he lifted the machine as though it weighed nothing and slammed it into the ground. Metal crumpled and shattered under the force.

The hairless one whimpered, struggling to drag himself away. His effort was futile.

Aluk advanced, his eyes cold. His massive hand reached down, cutting off the hairless one's final, strangled scream.

When the forest fell silent once more, the brothers walked back toward the clearing.

The red-breath still burned faintly, casting flickering light across the remains of the deer carcass the hairless ones had stolen from the woods. Aluk crouched beside it, running his massive hands over the animal's body. Its spirit belonged to the forest, not to the hairless ones who had taken it without care or honor.

With a series of deliberate gestures and vivid shared images, Aluk, and Matto came to an agreement: the deer would not be left here to rot. Nor would the bodies of the hairless ones remain to poison the sacred ground.

Matto hoisted the deer across his shoulder with ease, its lifeless form dangling against his broad back. His gaze lingered on the thunder stick lying in the dirt, its metal surface gleaming faintly. With a deliberate motion, he bent down, picked it up, and secured it alongside the deer. He had no idea what he was going to do with the weapon, but he knew he couldn't leave it behind for other hairless ones to find and use.

Aluk carried the bodies of the two hairless ones, their weight inconsequential against his immense strength. The brothers cast a final glance at the campsite and disappeared into the forest.

****

As the first light of dawn painted the horizon, the brothers returned to the sanctuary. Matto laid the deer at the center of the main cave, where it would be divided among the clan. Aluk turned to face the Elder, his chest heaving with the weight of his anger and pride.

The Elder's amber eyes flicked from the bloodied brothers to the deer and back again. Aluk's shared images depicted the events: the hairless ones stealing what was not theirs, the loud machine ravaging the land, and the brothers' swift retribution.

The Elder's expression remained unreadable, but his thoughts were firm. *You have acted without permission. You risked exposure.*

Aluk's response came quickly, sharp, and unrelenting: We protected the forest. *The hairless ones are no longer. The deer is ours again.*

Matto added his agreement, showing an image of the clan gathered around the deer, nourished by what had been stolen. *This is our duty. To guard. To provide.*

The Elder stared at them for a long moment before turning toward the depths of the cave. His final thought was projected to the whole clan: *You have risked more than you know. But tonight, the forest has been restored.*